A WALK DOWN BULLET ALLEY

BRONCO HAMMER

SIERRA WEST BOOKS

SWB editorial and review team
Holli Lawton
Mike Ratke
Randy Lewis
Jeff Trapp

Then out spake brave Horatius,
the Captain of the Gate:
"To every man upon this earth
Death cometh soon or late.
And how can man die better
than facing fearful odds,
For the ashes of his fathers,
And the temples of his Gods."

Lays of Ancient Rome

LORD THOMAS BABINGTON MACAULAY (1834–1838).

BOOKS BY BRONCO HAMMER

PRE-READ BRIEFING

Okay, everyone assemble, find a seat, and let's get ready to start another action-packed, hard-boiled mystery briefing. I'll keep this short.

Pack your bags, loyal readers, for a trip to sunny Florida. We're going to take on a case involving Russian organized crime, terrorists, stolen gold, and, of course, murder.

In this story, an aging private eye takes on a job that might well be his last.

As in all my books, there will be plenty of pointless violence, extreme action, and random explosions. So, even though this is in a new venue with new characters, I think you will find everything you expect from a Bronco Hammer book.

Remember to always have a cocktail, a gun, and a helmet with you when reading one of these literary masterpieces. We say 'danger is our business' for a very good reason.

Thanks for being a customer,

Bronco Hammer

PROLOGUE

Some days you win. Some days you lose. And some days you dig a bullet out of your belly fat with a pocket knife, then sanitize the wound with a splash of vodka.

Today was one of those days, and I noticed one important thing that you might want to write down.

The older you get, the harder this shit gets.

And my day started out so well, too.

Sit down and I'll tell you how this deal went south.

Just don't make any sudden moves.

CHAPTER 1

Lauderdale By The Sea, Florida

It was barely seven in the morning and the damp tropical air was already warmer than I wanted it to be. Oh, it's no surprise. I knew it would be hot. I also knew it would get hotter. Heat is inevitable. That's how it is around here... hot, humid, and bright... unless it rains. Then it's hot, humid, and wet.

I parallel parked the ragtop into a tight space directly in front of my regular coffee joint, backing in all the way and then squaring up, centering between the white pavement markers with just two quick turns of the steering wheel like a professional... I suppose because I *am* a professional.

Being old simply means it isn't as easy to twist the body and look over one's shoulder as it might have been twenty years ago, or even ten years ago, especially in the Jaguar. But I can still out drive most people on my worst day. All those years on the police driving track teaching pursuit operations, including high-speed backing, stick with you.

But I'm not a cop anymore. I retired so long ago that the academy recruits who started when I pulled the pin are all retired now too. Twenty-five years as a private snoop kept me in the game, but it's not the same thing.

I'm not complaining. Having things '*not being the same* 'is a blessing and certainly not a misery. Eventually you get tired of kicking doors, blowing up crack houses, and duking it out with punks in alleys.

Who am I kidding?

You never get tired of that stuff.

But your body does.

And that is the axiom.

It's an outcome which we all face.

Any man of action, be it cop, soldier, Marine, sailor, cowboy, spy, lumberjack... or any other old-school American hard-ass who's work attire qualifies them for a job with the Village People will understand my point without further discussion.

But today I am no longer a man of action. I'm an old man, a private detective who is set in his ways. Action for me now is reduced to getting up early, driving to the diner, and getting a cup of coffee.

So here I am.

But because my day will extend past a trip to the diner, I don't want mere mortal coffee. I need real coffee, and I am particular about what kind of coffee I drink. No, I don't go for the fancy stuff with an Italian name and stupid hints of random aromas. I like a heavy mug of black coffee, coffee that is strong enough to knock a starving buzzard off a rotting hog.... coffee that slaps you across your kisser and says, '*Good morning, asshole. Welcome to the shit show.*'

Ernie's Cafe makes that kind of brew and also a passable version of a pancake, even though Ernie didn't know what the hell a pancake was ten years ago when he came here from Croatia... or one of those places.

Wherever Ernie is from, he's like the Cubans. He came here to work, not for a free ride.

I could see from my car that the joint wasn't crowded yet... it would be packed by eight when the pussies of the world start moving.

I turned off the ignition, snatched my newspaper and hat off the passenger seat, carefully checked for traffic, got out of the car, and approached the entrance of an establishment which is formally named 'Lauderdale-by-the-Sea Breakfast and Lunch

Cafe. 'I think the name is too long. I'm not alone in that opinion. Everyone just calls it Ernie's cafe. Being part of everyone, I call it Ernie's Cafe too.

I stood at the edge of the door for a second to let my eyes adjust to the interior light. It's an old habit. The truth is, you don't want very good lighting in a place like this... file that information under *'what you can't see, won't give you food poisoning.'*

Ernie had three people seated at the counter. There were empty stools enough for six or seven more.

The joint was long and narrow. It had a few tables-for-two against one wall and a dozen stools wrapped in worn and duct taped red vinyl along the well-used counter that separated the diners from the cook, who typically worked with his back to the customers. Like a lot of diners in this part of the country, it was decorated with nautical stuff, seashells, and pictures of parrots. I don't know why everyone has parrot stuff. They should have iguanas. That intrusive species outnumbers parrots now about a million to one. And don't get me started on alligators. I hate those things. I don't know why, but they creep me out. I'm not a fan of lizards and snakes.

I edged inside the doorway.

The owner spotted me. Ernie was a noodle-armed little guy with a paper chef hat over his unkempt black hair and a pencil mustache that went out of style during the silent movie era.

"Sit down, sit down, my friend," Ernie gushed, encouraging me to come in and take a seat.

Friendliness is a highly overrated characteristic. It is about as welcome to me as discovering a case of the galloping dandruff in your undershorts.

I grunted a curt 'hello 'and took the stool that was furthest from the other customers. I could still monitor the front and back door while keeping my gun side shielded from any potential threats.

"Mister Becker," he pleasantly continued as he passed me a

menu that I didn't need. "How come you always wear a black suit and hat? We're in Florida. It's hot out."

The only thing I hate more than friendliness is a personal question asked by some turd I've barely known for eight years. I kept my answer to the point. "I'll take a coffee and some pancakes… butter the hell out of them. Two slabs of bacon."

He wrote my order on a pad and handed it off to the grill man, who nodded, reached for a plastic pitcher of batter, and splashed the mixture on the grill, creating three perfect circles of sizzling deliciousness. He tossed a couple of hunks of bacon on the grease bed alongside the three golden discs of delight.

The owner wasn't as fascinated with the grill cook's art as I was. He turned back facing me and started yapping again. "Becker, why you never talk.. you just say hello and make an order?"

"You have a cheerful smile, Ernie."

He grinned widely, "Why thank you, Mister Becker."

"I wonder if that smile would still be so cheerful with a fat lip and some missing teeth?"

'Huh?"

"Just bring me my pancakes and no more small talk. I like you, Ernie, but not very much." I pulled a handkerchief out of my interior jacket pocket and wiped my brow, a move that allowed the butt of the .45 automatic in my shoulder holster to peek out and say, '*go away now.*' Figuratively speaking, of course.

"You got it, Mister Becker," he replied nervously, now recognizing that he pushed a dangerous man too far with his pleasant bullshit. I'm not a morning person. I'm active in the morning. I'm simply not nice in the morning.

Ernie made a lemon sucking face while slowly backing away to engage in some nervous small talk with a more affable chap whose fat ass was parked on a stool at the opposite end of the counter.

I have no idea why Ernie is always so friendly. It makes me nervous. If you allow people to just start talking to you once, they always think it's okay to try it again. Nobody wants that.

I placed my newspaper on the counter and started trying to find the five or ten percent of the printed pablum that was actually news and then ferret out the two percent of the news that was remotely accurate.

An article caught my eye on the page dedicated to local stories.

Interesting.

A body was fished out of the intracoastal, which is not unusual. The body was the worldly remains of a guy I knew, which *is* unusual.

Charles Brookline Schuster seemed to have applied for a job as alligator bait, or maybe crocodile bait... I don't know. Just pick either one of those scary dinosaurs that love snacking on decaying flesh. I can't tell the difference. I just know I despise them. Although, if it turns out that they killed Schuster, I'll reassess my opinion.

According to this story, which was probably inaccurate, my former client was found naked and might have been the victim of foul play.

The last time I saw Schuster was two years ago. He was an annoying prick, always quoting that Airplane movie from the eighties. After forty years, those jokes get old. He stiffed me for a grand on a job. It was a finder's fee assignment to locate an asshole who stiffed him for five grand. I found the guy in four hours. A leather sap across the mouth helped him remember to take care of the debt.

The five grand was paid back. But Schuster went dark afterwards and never gave me my fee. I thought about breaking his leg for this gross display of poor judgement, but I realized I was getting too old to pull it off without risking a back injury, and the bastard wasn't worth the drama.

In this current news story, however, someone apparently determined that Schuster was worth the drama.

I decided I would check it out after breakfast, just for laughs.

There's nothing funnier than hearing about some guy who ripped you off being dead.

Still, there had to be more to it than that... besides, it wouldn't hurt to prove who did it before someone remembered that I had a motive to whack him. But it could wait until I wolfed down my pancakes.

Ernie directed the grill cook to deliver my cakes rather than serving me himself. For some reason, Ernie was very busy with something on the opposite side of the diner and was avoiding eye contact with me.

Good boy.

The cook slid an oversize plate with a three-stack and bacon my way. It came to a skidding stop immediately in front of me and my fork.

Perfecto!

I drowned those three golden-brown wretches in syrup and dabbed on some more butter from those little plastic butter cartons restaurants give you that hold less than a useable amount of butter per serving.

Delicious.

I took a bite of bacon. It was black, crispy, and was burned like a sinner doing a stretch in hell. Just the way I like it.

My day was looking up.

As a multitasker and small business owner, I made an executive decision to read and eat at the same time.

The grill cook glided by and topped off my coffee.

I found another story to read, but my thoughts kept drifting back to that bum Schuster.

Yeah, we weren't close, but I knew him well enough.

I took care of various jobs for Schuster over a period of about four or five years, with no problem. That last case, which, like I said, was two years ago, is the only one he ever stiffed me on. Schuster was a shifty bastard, but like most of the other shifty bastards I deal with, he was pretty honest until he wasn't. He fenced stolen property, mostly fine jewelry and gems. I had no part of his criminal enterprises, but I *did* collect some debts for him from time to time. He paid cash, always off the books, and he used to be reliable.

He liked me because I'm good at finding people, mean enough to make the right impression on errant screw-ups, and old enough to know how to keep my mouth shut.

I suspected this time he screwed with the wrong guy and got himself whacked... but I wanted to know more. I'm naturally curious like that.

I finished my meal and picked up the syrup-stained bill to check the damage. Thirteen-ninety-five. Reasonable for a tourist area. I tossed a twenty near my empty plate, picked up my paper, took a last slurp of coffee, adjusted the shoulder holster securing my old Sig Sauer Model 220 forty-five automatic, and headed back to the car.

The cook spouted his mandatory line as I hit the door. "Thanks and come back soon, Mister Becker."

I ignored the pleasantry. He didn't really mean it anyway. I didn't flip him off, which is just as good as an insincere *'thanks and have a nice day* 'reply.

I opened the door, tossed my fedora on the passenger seat, flopped my six-feet-one and two-hundred-and-thirty-eight pound geezer bod into the driver's seat, and then fired up the engine. If I gamed the traffic right, I could be at Schuster's office in ten minutes.

I love America. A country where a motivated individual can just do stuff because they feel like it.

The Warehouse District

There was plenty of parking directly in front of Schuster's warehouse, but I parked two buildings down just in case. My upscale car didn't match the downscale locale, so it was best to keep it out of sight.

I put my hat on and walked over to the entrance, projecting

confidence and purpose, looking very much like I was not up to some nefarious shit.

As I got to the door, I was surprised to encounter a uniformed private security guy standing guard. He stepped out of an alcove and stopped me. He was about five-feet-four and might have weighed in at around two bills or more. The guard sported some nice wrap-around style mirrored sunglasses, a blue helmet, and enough tactical gear to invade Nicaragua. I guess someone hired him to watch the place after Schuster got whacked, which was fine. I am always prepared for these contingencies.

Step one, flash the retired cop badge so fast that they only see it's a shiny yellow badge and nothing else. Two, pull fake documents while spouting off official sounding garbage about some important job I'm doing while exaggerating the authority I have to carry my assignment out.

The guard started our dance of the wills with a stern warning. "Sir, this building is closed," the guard announced as he gave me his best *'don't screw with me'* deterrent face.

Nice try, but I remained undeterred. I dialed up the old bullshit generator to eleven and took my turn at spreading manure. "My name is Inspector Kennedy." I announced authoritatively. "I'm from Building Inspections. I have a court order to inspect this warehouse, and I am charged with the duty of executing said order by the court." I pulled the phony court order I always keep in my interior suit coat pocket, a page of onerous ultra-fine-print gobbledygook narrative printed underneath a bold and gargantuan heading, 'COURT ORDER.' The document content might be vague, but the words 'court order 'were large, clear, and bursting with intimidation. If anyone ever bothered to read it, they would find that the faux court order provided the bearer with authority to do damned near anything, at almost any place, and at any time of my choosing. Nobody has ever challenged me on my fraudulent document in all my years as a cop and a private nose. I also made sure the guard noticed the big automatic hanging in my shoulder holster as I held the document in his face too closely for him to read.

"Building inspector?" He asked, with a confused look on his bloated kisser. "You guys carry guns?"

"Damned right."

"Cool."

I always use the title 'building inspector 'as a cover because it's almost impossible to get anyone at building inspections to answer the phone, let alone answer a question, thus voiding any risk of having my story debunked. And no one knows exactly what they have the authority to do or not do.

I blathered on, spreading my professional verbal manure a foot deep. "Yeah, whenever a citizen dies who is involved with US Commerce or retail, we are required by law to inspect the building and document said inspection for the estate. It's all standard."

"I didn't know that."

"It's part of the Patriot Act. You're a patriot, right?" I challenged.

"Absolutely. I'm also a member of the Moose Lodge," he added proudly as he propped up his national security credentials with his Moose Lodge membership.

"Then let's get this over with," I commanded with a thumbs up. "I have an appointment with the governor in an hour about illegal terrorism."

"Wow!" He returned the thumbs up, then started fumbling through a huge key ring containing approximately all the keys in the world. "This is like working with that 24 guy from TV!"

I kept talking as he fumbled so he wouldn't have time to think up a question that might shoot a hole in my story. "It's nothing really," I said modestly. "We all have to do our part." I gave him my grim but dedicated face that says, I'm doing my part.

He nodded in enthusiastic support. "I try to do my part too, sir."

"It shows. Now let me in so I can get to work."

"Yes, sir… no problem."

The chubby little security man couldn't open the door fast enough for me. Authority, real or imagined, when presented confidently, works wonders.

As I walked inside, the man grimly asked, "Do you need any help in there?" He assumed an unintimidating, yet determined stance, as if he was fully prepared to go in with me.

I think he was expecting we would encounter a battalion of Al Qaida terrorists inside, lurking in ambush, and that an imminent but glorious death was in the cards.

I let him off the hook. "No, thanks. Just make certain I am not disturbed. And if anyone else shows up, please give me a shout. I appreciate your service to security." I gave him a manly brother-in-arms shoulder punch, but not too hard. I didn't want to injure him.

That last bit pumped him up a little. He sucked in his gut and gave me a little salute.

Time to go in.

I did a quick scan about the musty warehouse, which was more of a long and narrow storage structure, with steps leading to an office loft in the back. The joint stank of mustiness and larceny. The warehouse area was lined with ancient steel shelving holding stacks of imported junk from China and other random shit that was probably hijacked from a truck or stolen in a commercial burglary. But I noticed the merchandise had not been touched for a while, as if it was abandoned some months ago. Perhaps for a more lucrative deal? The dust was thick and gross. Yeah, all these racks of crap were forgotten business. Something better must have come along.

My interest was focused on the office.

I climbed the stairs.

I could hear my knees.

They hate me.

Stairs seem steeper than they used to.

The office door was locked. I pulled my Spyderco knife out of my pocket, flicked open the blade, and popped the latch.

The office was about ten by fourteen feet in size adorned with vomit green paint on the walls, two steel file cabinets that were padlocked against the right side wall, stacks of cardboard banker boxes were on the opposing wall, and a big gray metal army surplus style desk centered in the room. Commercial designers might call this a 'mid-century industrial style. 'I call it a shitty looking office.

This is where things still happened... at least within the past couple of days. The warehouse area might have been abandoned, but the office showed signs of recent activity.

There was a cheap lamp on the desk, one of those goose neck deals made of plastic that was painted silver to look like metal. It had the worthless on and off switch built into the cord... definitely cheesy, but it worked. I flipped it on.

There was a old-school black landline phone on the desk that was heavy enough you could tether a hot air balloon to it. You don't see many of those anymore. Certainly no data stored in that thing to retrieve. I observed some papers scattered about on the desk. A quick inspection revealed the documents to be mostly garbage. I spotted more boxes of paperwork stacked in a far corner of the room behind the door. It reminded me of how people collect paper work they will never look at again, and after they die, the survivors will just toss it all in the trash. Hoarding paper is a common issue, fear of not having the information when you need it leads to this... my motto is, if it isn't important enough to remember, and if I can't fold it up and store it in my wallet, and if the cops aren't going to ask me for it, then I don't need it. But Schuster wasn't like that. He had reams of paper in his filing cabinets, desk drawers, and the boxes.

Well, he doesn't need it now.

For a moment, I thought about the shelving downstairs. A lot of empty space was available. He could have carried the boxes downstairs, wrote the date on them, and cleaned up his office. But I only thought about it for a moment because I recognized the thought as being stupid almost immediately. The boxes contained files he didn't want to risk some random warehouse worker seeing. Also, he was a slob and a lazy bastard.

Duh.

I like to search in unconventional places when I don't know what I'm looking for, under drawers, under rugs, behind bookcases. I found a few things in my time that way. Today was no different.

I found a pea-shooter, a little 22 automatic, hidden behind some books in the bookcase behind the desk. I also found a letter taped to the bottom of a metal folding chair leaning against the wall. It was an interesting letter. It was a 'to whom it may concern 'message.

I held it under the desk lamp to read the handwritten note...
'If I am found dead by suspicious circumstances, call Becker and tell him it was those guys from California. He will find them. Take in Grande, get to Pas.'

Well shit.

What the hell is he talking about? What guys from California? Who in the hell was this letter for? And why would Schuster think I would want to help avenge him? I'm happy he's dead, and he should have known I'd be happy he's dead.

You are a selfish dickhead, Schuster.

I stuffed the letter and gun in my pocket, worked my way carefully down the staircase, and made my way through the warehouse to the door.

"This day can't get any stranger," I grumbled.

I spoke too soon.

I'm a cautious man. When I don't know what's on the other side of a door, I take specific measures to make sure I don't get surprised. While I was waiting, it occurred to me the door was never alarmed. That seemed odd. Criminals often disconnect alarms, so cops don't accidentally show up at a bad time, but at some point, there was always some sort of an alarm installed in commercial properties.

I put my ear to the door and listened before opening it. My security guard was talking to someone. The conversation didn't sound hostile, but I couldn't clearly make out what was being said. It sounded like there might be more than one person speaking with the guard. I didn't like it, but I couldn't really wait it out either. I had things to do.

I overheard enough to determine it wasn't cops. It was somebody else. The killer? Maybe… so what, I don't really have a dog in this fight, just my cat-killing curiosity was at stake.

I put on my sunglasses and shaded my eyes so I wouldn't be blinded as I transitioned into the sunlight. I kept my gun hand free.

I casually stepped out into the bright Florida sunshine and oppressive heat.

Two clowns were chatting up mister security officer. One was sort of slender and very well dressed in expensive yet tasteful semi-casual attire, sporting a blue tropical tie and a lightweight dark blue sport coat with a colorful pocket square. The Persol shades had to have set him back about four hundred bucks. They were the real deal, not cheap knock-offs. His teeth had to cost a fortune. The complete set of implants gave him a movie star smile. He looked nice but not gay-nice, just tasteful, with a dapper, nicely trimmed beard, and a dark tan. Clown number two was a strikingly handsome Italian-looking guy except for an unfortunately bent nose. With his husky build, he might have been a high-school or college football lineman. His hands no longer bore perfect symmetry, so I'm guessing he had experience with manual labor or he punched a lot of people in his time. His bruiser charisma was obvious. Idiot number two wasn't as dapper as his pal. He dressed like some B-Movie hood in a black leather blazer, black jeans, silk t-shirt and cowboy boots. He was sporting a pair of Ray-Ban Wayfarers. Both had Rolex Submariners that looked legit. Bent-nose wore a gaudy gold diamond encrusted pinky ring.

Mobbed up? Unlikely…

Assholes? Definitely.

I knew instantly they were packing... I also knew they weren't from around here. How did I know? Experience... you just know after a while. I could see the weapon imprints in their clothing, the way they stood with their bodies slightly bladed like cops, the way they position their hands, their high level of confidence, all that explained how I knew about the guns.

Their accents and inappropriate clothing for the weather gave away that they weren't from around here. Although, who am I to talk? I am packing a 45 and wearing a black suit in ninety percent humidity and eighty-five degrees.

I pretended to ignore them as I addressed the security guard.

"Please secure the facility and keep my presence here confidential, as this is an active case. Thank you for your cooperation." I attempted to brush by and walk to my car, hoping to avoid any further discussion.

Bent nose stepped in front of me, "Hey, who are you supposed to be?"

Security guy, completely forgetting my confidentiality warning, answered the question, "This is the building inspector... routine in these cases," he blathered authoritatively.

I entered the fray before the guard screwed things up worse. "This is government business. Who in the hell are you two supposed to be?" Always answer a question with a question. Always counter a false accusation with a worse accusation. And always respond to a true allegation with at least three extremely offensive counter-allegations and an attorney.

The dapper guy inserted himself into the pending quarrel. "I'm a private investigator... from California... investigating a confidential matter for a client."

Bent nose spouted off too, "I'm his cousin, Johnny Dedd."

"Johnny who?" the guard and I asked at the same time.

"Sorry sir, he meant to say that he's my associate. We're from the Joseph Tucker Investigative Agency of Los Angeles. You might have heard of us."

I hadn't heard of them. Usually, upon hearing the word 'California,' I tune out any and all subsequent conversation. But this was business. "So what the hell do you and your *'cousin'* want? I already warned you that this is government business. Are you trying to get arrested, or are you just a couple of stupid fuckers?"

Shit. I let them get under my skin. A real building inspector probably wouldn't call someone a stupid fucker right off the bat. At my age, I should know better. But I don't. I never got used to taking shit or slick talk from anyone, and I probably never will.

While bent-nose focused on shaking a Lucky Strike out of a pack and lighting it, dapper guy answered my question with a bit more finesse, "I'm sorry this is getting off on the wrong foot, sir. I'm Joe Tucker, private investigator, and like I said, we're looking into a matter for a client. Perhaps we can start over and chat for a few minutes." he put out his paw in an offer to shake hands.

So I have a peacemaker and a troublemaker... basically a couple of turds from California, like we need more of those here. Reluctantly, I accepted the handshake. I noticed his hand was soft and his nails were manicured. Dedd was definitely the goon of the pair. I surmised that Tucker was a bit of a puss.

"You say you have a client?" I asked, rather than introducing myself. It wasn't time for that yet.

Tucker seemed more affable than Dedd... but both were clearly a couple of goofy nimrods. Typical California ass hats.

Tucker said, "Yes, confidential, of course, but there was a connection to a man who I believe was the owner of this building."

Mister Security guy stepped in to the chat, "Sir, don't you have to be on your way to meet the governor? I can deal with these two gentlemen for you."

I saw Tucker's eyebrow lift upon recognizing the load of crap I sold the security guard for what it was.

I had already forgotten that I made that nonsense up. Old age and a brain overstocked with decades of wisdom and knowledge will do that to you. Oh well, go with the flow. I needed to check out these two before I said anything further anyway.

"Yes, thank you. I'll have to be going gentlemen… I'm afraid this building is quarantined until the direct and proximate cause of death can be determined. There has been a rare tropical virus from Peru reported as infecting persons in the area, so I'm afraid you'll have to come back in two weeks after quarantine."

At this point, it was obvious that both of them knew I was lying my ass off. Maybe they weren't as stupid as they looked. They proved they weren't total idiots by sustaining my cover in front of the guard. It was the smart move to go with. A lie can be as revealing as the truth. Old detectives know this dictum to be factual.

"No problem," Tucker calmly stated as he handed me a card. "Please call me if you get a chance."

I could tell he was studying my face for a reaction. He didn't get one.

Dedd said nothing. He was distracted with a stare down against a giant green iguana that was chilling out in a little strip of grass between the buildings, doing some lizard push-ups. I don't think Dedd cared for lizards. He appeared uncomfortable with our local dinosaur-ancestor population. I can't say that I'm crazy about them either.

I took the card, grunted an acknowledgment, and disappeared myself around the corner. I didn't want them spotting my car. Seeing the luxury convertible would cause them to be even more curious. I found a place to duck into and waited them out.

It was going to be one of those kinds of days.

CHAPTER 2

Ten minutes later, I was back in my Jaguar and on the street, cruising north up Ocean Drive towards Lauderdale by the Sea.

I had a lot to think about on the way to my office. Dead ex-friend. Dead ex-friend's cryptic message about a killer from California. Gun I just stole from dead ex-friend's office. Two dumb shits from California showing up out of the blue. Sandwiches…. yeah, I was hungry again. That pancake stack just didn't get the job done. A big man requires big fuel.

I whipped into a local tiki bar / diner joint on the beach for an early lunch. The out-of-town crowd was light, and the working locals wouldn't be lining up for chow in any numbers for another hour.

I took a small two-seat table by the sidewalk so I could people watch… I enjoy watching the tourists and the locals going about their daily business. Each scene is a story, and each story ends with 'Florida is nice but it's so hot and humid.'

I spotted my first piece of entertainment, silently marching eastbound to the sea.

The pale-skinned guy in the white socks, sandals, tank top, and Cincinnati Reds baseball cap was absolutely a tourist. It was obvious that he hadn't taken his shirt off outdoors in at least eleven years. His chunky wife's clothing revealed far too much skin for her generous figure. She was as pasty-white as he was. They were walking hand-in-hand towards the beach. By late this afternoon, they would both be as orange as a Cincinnati Bengals uniform. Later, they would be strolling by here again in the opposite direction to celebrate a double-case of severe sunburn at their hotel.

A couple on the corner were definitely locals. They were dressed for the weather, tan, not taking in any sights, no posing for photos. He had on loose light green slacks and flip-flops with a plain T-shirt. No need for logos. She was in a short skirt, and spaghetti strap top with a wide-brim but tasteful straw sun hat on her head. The woman was also a very dark tan.

Then there was the nasty old New Yawker... Overdosing on gold jewelry, spouting off about his observations in a loud voice as if he thought everyone would want to hear what he had to say, walking like he owned the joint, and sporting a healthy serving of disdain for all things non-New York painted across his face. I could hear him explaining something about 'the city' to his much younger money grubbing slut-charisma girlfriend. Was I being too judgmental? Nah, I could see in her face she was calculating how soon this knob might die, but her love of money outweighed the hatred of her current circumstances. I envision a well-compensated pool-boy in her life.

That was just a twenty-second take of the street scene near the beach.

I love Florida.

I've never taken the time to confirm or disprove my observations, but if I was a gambling man, I'd bet I'm right one-hundred percent of the time. Being a cop does that to you. You develop special skills in quickly assessing any situation, placing a life story around each person involved, and then acting accordingly. Once in a while, you misjudge one, but only while you are a rookie. That particular super-power is enhanced exponentially over time.

An old cop can walk into a room full of people and, more likely than not, be able to cough up a description and a back-story for everyone in the place the next day. The process is simple; one, identify all threats, two, identify all parties with criminal intent, three, identify all hot members of the opposite sex, and four, pick out the prey animals. That is basic survival. The alpha-predators might even acknowledge you with a respectful nod to let you know they mean you no harm. It's a professional courtesy. The prey animals will walk around cluelessly bumping into stuff, not recognizing that the criminals, predators, and the charmers who use weaponized sexuality are already mentally dividing up their stuff. The descriptions come with experience. You mentally map some clothing to a face, to a build, and tag each person with a one or two word tag... like knob, dirtbag, hottie, slob, beach bum, snot rag, puke face.... things that will help you remember them. What is amazing is that if you talk to another cop who was there and ask if they saw 'snot rag, 'they will know exactly who you meant.

I lit up a smoke while I waited for a fish sandwich, some fries, and a cola. The fish was grouper today. It was going to be fresh. It's almost always fresh around Fort Lauderdale. This establishment is particularly good. I gratefully inhaled that special essence of fish shack wafting through its atmosphere. The scent made me even more hungry.

Speaking of fish, I fished my little leather bound mole notebook out of my pocket and began scribbling down some additional thoughts on today's activities while they were still fresh in my mind.

Thought one, Schuster got whacked. Why?

Thought two, he expected to get whacked. Thus, the mysterious note. What made him expect it?

Thought three, he expected me to do something about it. Note to self; review personal notes about curiosity killing cats and old detectives.

Thought four, I'd need to figure out who that note taped to the chair was intended for. There was another name to uncover.

And thought five, I'd have to find out what those two turds from Cali were up to. Did they kill Schuster? If so, I'd either have to kill them both or buy them each a beer in gratitude... the jury was still out on that one.

So, having committed my thoughts to paper, I gave myself thirty seconds to consider what it all means.

I only needed five of those seconds. What it means is simple. I'm taking on a new case called 'who murdered Schuster and why do I give a shit.' That's the case. A dead guy is the client and I'm the consulting detective.

Lucky for me I don't need money or this would be a massive waste of time and resources... but I'm curious, and curious people like me need to know things... I needed to know who whacked Schuster.

Time for grouper.

All this thinking has left me famished.

CHAPTER 3

Offices Of Becker Investigations

Although I don't flaunt it publicly, I live very well. I'm not a stereotype retired cop turned two-bit private nose who lost his pension and is broke from three ugly divorces. I'm the opposite of broke. I have a generous pension, and I was never divorced. But that doesn't mean I don't carry a heavy burden on my soul. The hollow comfort wealth brings isn't worth the price I paid for it.

When my wife passed, she left me a pile of cash. Being a man of old-fashioned ideals when I was younger, I insisted on supporting us, even though I knew she came from a family with some significant money. We didn't get along. I thought I knew it all. They actually *did* know it all. They didn't get rich by being stupid. But one thing that I didn't see coming was her setting up a big fat trust fund for me. I didn't know about it until the end. I remember her telling me at the hospital, don't spend it all in one place, Becker.

She laughed. It was the last wise-crack she ever dropped on me. It was the last time I heard her laugh. She was always quick-witted and funny. It was a big part of why I loved her.

She punctuated her laughter with a wink.

I just faked a smile.

It's hard to laugh in a hospital room with a clock ticking, reminding you that each passing second is gone forever.

She made sure I'd have a comfortable life. She was right. But it was empty as hell without her in it. But very comfortable. By comfortable, I mean what wealthy people call comfortable. At the end, she had no living relatives or heirs other than me. She didn't trust charities. Too many of them were money laundering schemes or tax shelters, with very little going to the poor. So I wound up with a big estate and trust fund.

Money does not equate to solace.

This office, the condo, the investments, the car, they would all be gone in a second for just a little more time with her.

I lit a cigarette to break the melancholy. The snap click sound of the lighter focuses me. Maybe that's why I smoke too much. Ten years later and my mind still goes there, every damned day.

I appreciate my luxury office on an intercostal canal, the Jaguar convertible, the beautiful waterfront condo, multiple bulging bank accounts, but the middle-class neighborhood house we shared in Coral Gables was home until the damned doctor gave us the long face.

I looked out the window over the boatyard. Men were working on a forty-footer, a nice cruiser. I missed the ancient eighteen-foot boat we had, but it held too many happy memories. I sold it and got something newer, more sterile… it's just a boat, not a memory.

I guess life ain't all dolphins and mojitos, my friend.

Maybe I'd call my drinking buddy Maggie and see if she wanted to have a beer later. She always says if I'd just let go of the past, she'd make a happy man out of me. But I'm not ready to let go. I just want someone to have a beer with once in a while who isn't actively trying to kill me. That's all I need at this point. Maybe someday that might change. Not today. Maggie's years as a prosecutor specializing in insanity defense cases made her an interesting pal… but just a pal… right now…

It was time for a long drag on my cigarette, followed by a floating smoke ring full of disappointment and could-have-beens. Exhale it all out. Let it go. Let that shit go.

I got out of my chair and made a cup of coffee. Time to kick the misery out of my soul and get to work. Work keeps life pure.

It filters out the anguish and backfills the hole with purpose.

I flavored the coffee with a dash of Jack and took it with me as I wandered out to the teak wood exterior deck to watch the workers. I needed to think. I needed to think about Schuster.

I pulled the message out of my pocket. *California…* it was no coincidence those two half-wits were here. But who did Schuster know in California? And why would someone from across the country be interested in a two-bit jewelry fence? Did he off some fake '*merch*' to the wrong guy? Not likely. He was a professional. It had to be something else. And who was this note meant for? I guess I could start there. Who in the hell gave a shit about Charles Brookline Schuster?

I wandered back inside behind my desk and plopped down in my custom leather office chair. I opened the notebook computer and typed an email to Dourdhoff Jenkins, my designated computer research dude. For two-hundred buck a pop, he would find out everything about anybody and, most times, deliver the complete contents of their hard-drive to me at no additional charge. I saved his ass once in a little misunderstanding with the government, so he makes sure I get the platinum level service. I've known this idiot since high school. We called him Durd the Turd, because he was such an obnoxious know-it-all. We didn't realize then that he was about ten times smarter than our entire crowd of losers put together. We all liked sports and partying. He liked technology, design, and engineering… turns out he was cooler than us after the technology boom hit.

I reconnected with him during a federal case in which he was listed as an unindicted co-conspirator. I guess it's safe to call him an acquaintance now. I hate to get too chummy with anyone. But we have lunch together about once a month and discuss politics, classic professional wrestling, and wristwatches. He's a dedicated luxury watch aficionado, and I'm more of an enthusiast. I enjoy wearing my new Santos sports watch or the gold Royal Oak Offshore when I'm not sporting my G-Shock or my Islander. I dig the little five-o'clock logo on those. He's got some cash invested in a variety of very high-end luxury watches, but he only wears Patek. He must have ten of them. The computer crime business pays well. He's even richer than me.

My typing is woefully slow... punching too many heads in your youth leaves arthritis in the knuckles as you get older... if only back then I knew that an appropriately delivered open hand slap would have sufficed, I wouldn't have damaged my fists on all those hard skulls.

... Dourdhoff, I need all info available intelligence on family, close associates, enemies, and friends, if any, on Charles Brookline Schuster of Fort Lauderdale, Florida... W/M approximately 50 years old, jewelry fence, dirtbag, and asshole. If you need further description, please advise...

Send.

Okay, that part was done.

I'd have to talk to the two Californians next, but not until after I know more than they know.

Step one, call their office.

Three rings and what sounded like a lady who was a life-time smoker answered.

"Tucker Investigative Agency, Deb speaking."

"Yes, I'm from LA County Today magazine and we are considering doing a story on the owner of the business. Can you give me a little background, please?"

"One moment."

I heard her speaking to someone at her end. It sounded as if the other person's name was Stump... can that be a real name?

A man's voice came on the line.

"Who the fuck is this again?"

This guy sounded more like a bag man than a private detective.

I continued my ruse. "LA County Today magazine... I'm the editorial director and we were considering doing a story on the Tucker Investigative Agency."

"Bullshit... nobody would write about Tucker. He's a puss... now a good story would be... get out your pencil... ready?"

"Sure, go ahead."

"A good story would be '*go fuck yourself.*' Now, who is this and what do you really want?"

My ruse was working perfectly.

"Fine, you got me... I had to try. Look, I'll be perfectly honest. I'm working accounts receivable from the Indigo Jewelry Store downtown. Tucker owes us twelve hundred bucks for a watch service on his Submariner. It's two months overdue for payment. I thought if I could find out where he was, I could go over and ask him for the money face to face."

"Well, you're shit out of luck, pal. One, Tucker doesn't have any money, and two, he's in Florida on a case."

"Oh... I was hoping I could get this collected. He was referred to us by another customer, a Mister Deddario... am I pronouncing that right? He bought a Submariner from us to some time back."

"Dedd... He actually pays his bills. He's not a puss like Tucker, but Dedd isn't the sharpest pencil in the box. He's in Florida with Tucker."

"Shit... so Tucker is a legit detective?"

"Yeah, he's got a license, but he's leaves all the work for the rest of us. He's a real knob. I'm not surprised he stiffed you. I handle his money. Come by and I'll give you a grand cash to settle it... does that number work?"

"Sounds good, thanks. What's your name again?"

"Just ask for Mister Stump."

"Would you be interested in a nice Rolex or Omega?"

"I have a Timex Marlin on my wrist I've been wearing since 1978... why do I need some overpriced Swiss bullshit to tell me what time it is?"

"So, perhaps a nice Hamilton or Tissot?"

"Fuck you."

"Got it, thanks."

I disconnected. That went well. I learned early on in my investigative career that if you are going up against somebody who is street smart, let them think they outwitted you first, then they tend to give up information to keep you in your place in the pecking order.

Stump was good. I certainly wouldn't consider crossing him. He sounded like he was an older man and had some experience. But even the best fall for the old '*shit you got me* 'ruse, at least over the telephone... I suspected that if he had eyes on somebody, he'd see through any lie or deception instantly.

So, I know I have a match on my Rolex observation at the warehouse, so that means that the guy who handed me the business card was probably Tucker. I know Tucker is kind of a puss. It was obvious. He's probably tougher than most guys, but is nevertheless a bit of a dandy. I also know for certain now that Dedd is bad news, but I sensed that immediately. I know Tucker's agency is doing well enough to have a receptionist and a goon on staff at the minimum, maybe more. I also now know he's a legitimate private investigator, and he is here on a case.

My computer made that stupid ding sound, announcing I had received an inbound email.

It was Dourdhoff.

Things were moving fast.

He sent a pile of attachments, which I would print out and take with me. Some of them were Schuster's emails, some were public records, some were government records... possession of most of this crap could probably get me arrested for some kind of wire fraud or computer crime. It would be a shame to go down on some technical crime after my record of busting heads.

I grinned at the irony... or would that be incongruity?

It didn't matter.

Last year I wisely invested in a high-speed top-quality printer, so I just started making hard copies of each attachment. The machine cranked them out amazingly fast. I recalled the days of pulling those side-things with the holes off of each page when you printed something... and the noise... Shit. We thought that was a miracle device back then. Now this thing can silently print a book in five minutes. Sometimes progress doesn't suck.

I made a bathroom run, checked my mailbox, and poured a cup of coffee. When I returned, the printer was done. I noticed it had a light blinking a message that I needed more paper. I'd put an order in online.

The pile of paper on the tray was complete. It was about two inches thick. I put all of it into one of those big yellow document envelopes with the red thread and button deal. I could read the file at my next stop. The problem with big files is that sometimes important details are lost in the volume of data.

I stopped and lit a cigarette. Whenever I think about a phrase like *volume of data*, I feel like I'm closer to being a computer guy... smart, detail oriented, able to get my remote control for the TV to work... It might be fantasy, but sometimes you got to stop and smell the roses. It's the little things that make life worth living.

Also, I had to remember basics. It would be easy to be caught up in the California connection and blow off the boring basics of interviewing everyone I knew that Schuster also knew. But I talk to those people all the time. The California connection was interesting, something different. There was something compelling about a couple of assholes from the west coast nosing around a murder case. I'd try to stay focused. After all, I'm almost kind of a computer guy now. I think a lot about stuff like volume of data.

I finished my smoke.

I left the office and swung by my condo. Not everybody can afford to live oceanfront. I can, but I prefer the Intracoastal. The ocean is nice, but the Intracoastal gives me a backyard facing west for sunsets. Sunrises are overrated. And there is more to look at on the intercostal. The ocean has the nice wave crashing sound, but the action is on the waterway.

My place was a modest two-story three-thousand plus square foot condo with a private garage for my Jaguar. The condo had a boat dock, where I docked my thirty-seven foot Edgewater center console, and a private waterfront patio with a hot tub and a deck above it that provided me shade downstairs and a place to walk out of my upstairs master bedroom with a cup of morning coffee.

Some of my acquaintances had much more, and I could easily afford much nicer, but to me it was heavenly... except I wish she was here to enjoy it with me.

I switched into my off-duty threads, comfortable light blue cotton shorts, a dark blue designer polo, and some casual canvas shoes. I flipped my straw fedora on my head.

As I passed through the kitchen, I grabbed a twelve pack of Butt Whisker beer out of the SubZero refrigerator on my way to the patio.

I parked my ass in my favorite recliner and started sipping beer and reading the file.

A County Sheriff patrol boat came by. I know those guys well. Nothing like boat patrol as a cop. The marine detail lives a life almost as charmed as the fire department guys.

The pilot, Eric Thorson, spotted me and pulled up to the dock behind my Edgewater center console. Eric's last name was fitting. He looked like a Viking, a six-foot-four muscle-head with thick blonde hair.

"Hey Becker, you kill anybody today?" Eric yelled as a new guy hopped off the gunwale and tied off their vessel.

"I gave that violence shit up years ago, you pussy."

That made him snort.

"Like that guy you smoked in West Palm Beach last year?"

"He shot first, kid. That isn't like killing somebody. That's more like teaching someone manners."

Thorson introduced his partner, "Becker, this is Pete Charles. Charles, this is Becker. He's a mean old bastard."

I shook the kid's hand. "Nice to meet you."

"Nice to meet you, sir."

A polite kid. I liked that.

I pulled a couple of beers out of my current twelve pack. "Take these for the parking lot de-briefing after work."

Then I came to my senses.

"Take the whole twelve pack. I have more."

Eric grinned. "I'll only take it to prove I don't need a lesson in manners. Otherwise, this beer is confiscated in the name of public service. Just trying to protect an old fat detective from his bad habits."

That made *me* snort. "Hey Thorson, do you know why motor officers have TGIF stamped on their boots?"

"Thank God it's Friday?"

"No, Toes Go In First."

That made both of them laugh. Everybody loves a motor cop joke, at least all the other cops do.

"What are you working on?" Eric asked.

"I'm looking into who killed Schuster the fence. Did you know him?"

"No, I only worked patrol, SWAT, and this gig. Never did a stretch in property crimes or any other detective gig. But one of the guys on the marine detail was talking about it."

"Anything interesting?"

"They say he got tortured before they whacked him."

"Oh... revenge or professional?"

"Nobody knows... it looked more like low-tier professionals. At least that's what the guys were saying. Either way, it wasn't a good time for Schuster."

"Did he suffer?"

"Oh yeah."

"Too bad. Do you know where the body went?"

"Stand by, I'll phone my pal."

While Eric walked aside, chatting on the phone, I talked to the new guy. "Been on long?"

"No, four years. Since I was Navy with sea experience, I wound up over here. I had my Coast Guard Captain's license, so I guess they sent me where they needed me. That's kind of what I do. Go where I'm needed."

The kid had a pleasant way about him. He wasn't bragging, and he wasn't complaining. Just chatting. I didn't hate him.

He asked me a question next, probably out of politeness more than curiosity. "Eric said you were on the PD."

"Yeah, I probably retired before you were born. But I still have the PD blue blood pumping through my veins."

"I get it. My grandfather was a cop in California. His name was Jimmy Charles. He was a training officer. I think I inherited some of his blue blood in my veins. I just feel like I'm supposed to be doing this."

"I get it, kid. I totally get it."

It was nice to see a kid enjoying the job. True police work is an art form, and it should be enjoyed.

Eric came back with information.

"Schuster is still at the Medical Examiners. Nobody claimed him yet. They're still looking for a next of kin. There might be a daughter in California. But you know, women change their last names, people out west move around a lot... they aren't optimistic."

"If you can get that next of kin's name for me, there is a case of beer in it for you."

"Deal. I'll be over at the M.E.'s day after tomorrow on a floater case post-mortem. I'll see what I can dig up."

Radios started squawking. The new kid said something to Eric about a jet ski crashing into a hundred-foot yacht.

Thorson went back to cop mode. "Got to run, Becker. Talk to you later."

"Swing by anytime. There's always cold beer here."

I watched with more than a little envy as the crime fighters took off to deal with the shit that nobody else would deal with.

Police work.

I miss it.

I walked back into the house to get another twelve pack of beer since those two thieving pirates stole the last one. The dirty bastards. I chuckled under my breath as I thought about the old days, all my pals... now mostly dead. We usually don't last long after retirement. I beat the odds. Not sure if that is a blessing or curse. But still the memories make me laugh.

To be candid, I was grateful the young guys still came around and hung out. It is the best part of my day when that happens. They like to listen to stories of kicking ass in the old days, and I love hearing about the new stuff going on, which is a hell of a lot like the old stuff that went on except with cameras and less swearing.

Oh well.

I returned to my reading.

I found some interesting emails to and from Schuster. I don't know how Dourdhoff gets them, but you would think email would be more difficult to steal.

Item one, Schuster seemed to have offed some merch to a Los Angeles guy. The name of the buyer seemed familiar. The name wasn't familiar in a criminal way, but something else. Not Hollywood shit... but... sports.. some guy involved in a professional sports team. I wrote the name down in my notebook. The stolen property, or let's just say property since I don't know for sure it was stolen, was gold ingots. That was different. There might have been multiple prior transactions between the two of them the way the email read, but this one was two weeks ago.

Item two, Schuster had a birth certificate. Funny, I thought he crawled out from under a rock. But he was born in Los Angeles County, California and was fifty-nine years old. I thought he was younger. He must have had good genes, or he took care of himself. Now that I think about it, I've never seen him drink or smoke. The vital statistics data included a high school diploma from Torrence High... meh.

I opened another beer and lit a Lucky Strike before continuing with my file review.

Item three, according to the text messaged bank transaction reports, he deposited eight-hundred thousand into his bank accounts over the past two months.

Item four, on the night of his likely demise, he had a dinner date set with a lady named Jeanine Faraday. He'd been seeing her for a couple of months. She was apparently attracted to assholes. It doesn't say that in the file, it's just a deduction.

I put away the rest of the file for later and focused on beer and thinking.

Lots of California threads to pick at here. But I still don't know who that note was for or why he'd think I'd know what to do.

Maybe I'd sleep on it. Something would pop. Or maybe I could talk to the California Bobbsey Twins and see what they know. I feel like I have a good enough grip on this thing to talk to them now. I'd call Tucker in the morning. For now, it was hot tub time. I turned on some Sinatra, got a fresh beer, and boiled myself like a lobster. It felt great.

A big Sea Ray cruiser came down the canal. There was an older guy and a hotter younger woman with him. They waved as they passed. I waved back.

I decided to switch to Gentleman Jack on the rocks. The switch meant fewer bathroom trips later, and I'd be able to forget what I needed to forget sooner.

The Offices Of Becker Investigations

Another day at the office. I work alone, no receptionist, no assistants. I like it that way. It's simple. People have a way of weaseling into your life and complicating things. I don't need that drama in my life right now, or in the foreseeable future.

Outside in the boatyard, I could see their workers were still slogging away on that cruiser. I always felt that updating an old boat was wiser than buying the latest and greatest. The old ones had thicker fiberglass. They also had the smell of the sea soaked into them. Some people don't like that smell. I live for it.

I tossed the envelope full of documents on my desk and carefully placed my new black Goorin Nighthawk hat on the hatrack. The hatrack was one of my favorite pieces. It was from an old office building in Miami from the 1930s. My desk was an antique wooden writing table. I like real wood and pieces with real history... maybe it's an *old guy* thing. Eventually, my stuff will be back in style. I think the problem is designers. The old stuff was designed on function first and then beauty. Now they design things to make a statement. It must be the new generation's need to make sure everyone hears what they have to say rather than saying something everyone might benefit from hearing. If I were going to *make a statement* it would be *leave me alone and close the door on your way out.*

Luckily, we have a lot of wealthy people donating interesting things to the thrift stores around South Florida, so the old stuff can be found if you are willing to look for it.

I opened the window wide enough to get some salt air. It was a little cooler this morning. A squall might be heading our way. I made myself comfortable at the desk, that is, I undid the button on my trousers and propped my feet up on the corner of the antique desk top.

I thumbed through my notes, reviewing my thoughts before making the first call. I circled the note about remembering to work my local connections instead of getting wrapped up in this California drama. I can't get too far off track. But I need to know what they know.

I dialed the number from the business card I was given at the warehouse.

The voice I recognized from outside the warehouse came on line, "Tucker."

"Mister Tucker. We met yesterday. I think it might be of mutual benefit if we get together to talk about the late Charles

Brookline Schuster."

"Who is this again?" Tucker asked.

"I was introduced to you as Mister Kennedy, but I am a local private investigator. The name's Becker."

"Oh, I see. So... where and when, Mister Becker?"

His voice did not reveal any concern or interest... very professional for an idiot. Interesting.

"Anytime this morning." I gave him my office address.

"We'll be there in two hours. We'd come immediately, but my associate Mister Deddario is previously engaged until then."

"Fine. See you then."

I assumed Dedd was too hung over to function. I don't know why I thought that. I decided that if I had two hours to kill, I might want to run down the block to the little French breakfast joint. It wasn't as good as Ernie's, but it was good enough. I'm thinking scrambled eggs, bacon, potatoes, and some rye toast... or maybe an omelette. I'd decide on the walk over. Their coffee is delicious. I buttoned my pants, adjusted my shirttail, and headed that way.

I crossed Commerce and found an outside table. The blonde lady who owns the place took my order and then read it back to me in her thick French accent. She obviously wasn't 'Paris French, 'she was from rural France. There is a distinctive difference.

I chatted with her for a second in her native tongue. Speaking French was the only thing from high school that stuck with me. I should have taken Spanish, though. I know one local Brigitte Bardot and about a million Ricky Ricardos.

An hour later and with a delicious omelette consumed, I strolled back to my office. I left the office door ajar, placed the Sig 220 on the desk, and waited.

Ten minutes later, a knock on the doorjamb and a semi-quiet 'hello 'informed me that my guests had arrived.

"Come in."

Tucker came in first with Dedd right behind him. I noticed

Tucker was slightly breathless after ascending the single flight of stairs. My two-story office building doesn't have an elevator.

"Sit down." I pointed to the two wood and leather chairs in front of my desk.

Dedd looked like he was there to kill me. Tucker appeared cautious but friendly and spoke first. "Nice view."

"Thanks." I didn't move. I kept my facial expression frozen on grim.

Tucker and Deddario took seats. I didn't sense any threats, so, moving slower than a disgruntled postal service counter-worker on tax day, I put my weapon in a desk drawer. There was no sense in causing any unwarranted anxiety.

I began, "Now, let's talk. What are you guys looking for?"

Dedd wasn't in the mood to be interrogated. "That's our business... why should it be any of yours?"

That didn't go well.

I decided to de-escalate the tension. I carefully opened the bottom right desk drawer and removed a bottle of Jack and three glasses.

I poured.

Cautiously, I pushed two glasses towards my guests.

"To the thin blue line. Hook and book and don't look back."

I had them pegged as ex-cops and I was right. They couldn't refuse the toast. My hearing isn't as great as it used to be, but I'm pretty sure I heard Dedd whisper something that rhymed with 'other trucker 'under his breath.

Tucker took it differently. A smile and a sip followed by, "So, where were you on the job?"

I began the mandatory former-cop dialogue exchange.

"Here, but back in ancient history, Not Lauderdale-by-the-Sea, but Fort Lauderdale PD. I did SWAT, vice, fugitive apprehension, robbery suppression. All the fun stuff... how about you?"

Tucker began, "I was SWAT, patrol, a few years of burglary,

then I got shot in a liquor store hold-up and was medically retired."

Deddario got with the show-and-tell program next, "I was SWAT, narcs, vice, then they put in me in the persons crime detail and I murdered a child-molester in an interview room and went to prison." He stopped and stared to see how I would react.

In response to that revelation, I refilled his glass, this time to the brim. "Nice work."

That got a smile out of him. I think the three of us just bonded. I decided to lay my cards on the table. No sense playing games at this point.

"I'm looking into the torture and murder of an asshole I knew named Charles Brookline Schuster. I guess you could say he is my client." I tossed the mysterious letter he wrote onto the table. They read it and waited for the rest of my story. I decided not to tell them about the suspected gold digger, Jeanine Faraday, yet. She would be my wild card, besides she was a local matter at this point.

I continued, "I don't give a shit that he's dead, but I'm curious as to why… I'm curious about a lot of things with this case. Schuster was the owner of the warehouse you were at yesterday. He was a jewelry fence and a dick… that's about all I have."

"Interesting," Tucker replied. "We're working for a guy in Los Angeles who was ripped off for twelve million bucks. Our client is an asshole, but he pays cash. We were following a lead to the warehouse."

"Did your client whack him?"

"I don't think so," Deddario said. "Otherwise, he wouldn't have sent us. I think your guy Schuster was further down the rat hole. Someone higher up on his side probably did it, maybe someone from here."

"That makes sense. By the way," I directed at Deddario, "What do I call you, Dedd or Deddario?"

"On the streets of Los Angeles, people call me Johnny Dedd."

"What do they call you here?"

"Nobody called me anything yet. How should I know?"

I learned something just then. You need to be pretty specific when you discuss anything with Deddario. "Let me rephrase that. What do you *want* me to call you?"

"Johnny Dedd. What do I call you?"

"Becker. Everybody calls me Becker."

"Okay, Becker. That works for me."

We clicked cocktail glasses and drank on it. Finally, a breakthrough with the alpha male of the duo. I got to the point. "Look, I'll share what I got. I don't think we will be stepping on each other's toes... and I can provide local knowledge. You want to work together on this or part company? I'm good either way."

They glanced at each other and exchanged what looked like psychic approval. Dedd answered for them. "Sure, Becker. We'll work with you. My cousin already checked you out. It sounds like you killed more assholes here in south Florida than heart disease, shark attacks, and hurricanes combined. That is what I call quality police work."

I did a slight eye roll. I don't enjoy emphasizing the extreme violence that had been an integral part of my police career. But what Dedd alleged is true. I concluded it was now fair play to spill what I had on them.

"I know about you two guys, too. Tucker beat an armed robber to death with a twelve-pack of beer in Oxnard after getting shot to pieces... and Dedd, somehow you got a full pardon, PI ticket, and a gun license after being convicted of murder. That tells me you aren't pussies and you have some pull somewhere." I paused for a deep breath, then started again. "I know every dirtbag, every dope house, every robbery crew, every mobster, every peep show, shit show, sideshow, and I'm on a first name basis with every sleazy operator in South Florida. I can save you time on your case and you can help me satisfy my curiosity about Schuster. What can go wrong?"

Those turned out to be prophetic words.

CHAPTER 4

Dedd and Tucker agreed to my proposal. We were ready to proceed.

Tucker asked a cogent question, which I found pleasantly surprising. "What's your next move, Becker?"

The question revealed a deference to experience and demonstrated a degree of professional courtesy, which I appreciated. So I answered him. "I need to find a next of kin, or any close associate of Schuster. How about you?"

"We are looking for a guy who has gold... lots of gold... like bricks of gold, bullion, coins. Except we think about ninety-nine percent of it is scrap metal covered in gold paint. Someone scammed our client. He's pissed off. He invested in a scheme to process treasure secretly from an ancient shipwreck or something."

I interrupted. "Those scams are pretty common here."

Dedd said, "Our client didn't know that. He doesn't know much of anything. He's a trust fund baby. We have a lot of those in California."

"I hear you... it sounds a little like some of the West Palm Beach crowd. But how did you wind up at that warehouse?"

Dedd took the question. "We were just running down a phone number. The client said he received a call from that number. He was a little evasive about the details around the call, so we decided to check it out first. I don't trust that turd to give us a straight answer... but his checks clear, so there *is* that."

Business is business, I thought. I do private investigations more as a hobby rather than a job, and it helps me keep pretending like I have a reason to live. I wish I was like these two guys... not that stupid, but still in the middle of shit, digging for every buck to keep their business alive, living life. They don't realize how good they have it. Especially considering one should have died in the liquor store shoot out and the other should be serving life without the possibility of parole.

Focus, Becker.

I got my attention back on track. "So, he had a phone on his desk, an old land line. That was probably it. I scribbled the number on a scratch pad and handed it to Tucker."

"That's it. Maybe we should go back again and take another look."

"Not a bad idea. I'd like to get the guard out of the way, without hurting him, of course," I said.

Dedd looked a little sad when I suggested not hurting someone, but he said nothing.

Tucker made a suggestion, "I don't think they have twenty-four-hour guard service. We might be able to get in when the afternoon shift guy leaves."

"What about alarms?" Dedd asked.

"There wasn't one," I answered.

"Seems unusual in a place like that," Tucker commented.

I frowned. "Yeah, and it tells me that warehouse wasn't the site of the genuine show... it's somewhere else."

Dedd agreed and added, "We definitely need to go back there to find our connection."

"Let's hit it tonight. Hopefully, the guard won't be there. We can see what we can see," Tucker said.

"Agreed. You two swing by here around eight. We'll case the building and decide how to make a move on it. I have a lock pick so we're good to go."

Dedd said, "I have to pick up a few things first."

"Do you need help finding anything?" I asked, offering my local expertise, but also curious as to what '*things*' he thinks he might need.

"No, what I need shouldn't be too hard to find. We'll be ready."

We finished our drinks and the two L.A. guys went back to their hotel, or at least that's where they said they were going. I went home for a nap.

Sunset At The Warehouse

It was dark out, and the industrial area was poorly lighted.

We did a drive-by on Schuster's warehouse in their rental car.

Dedd was scooted down in the back seat, covertly eyeballing the place as Tucker and I gazed ahead.

"There's a uniformed guard there, not the same guard we talked to."

Shit.

I decided it wasn't all bad news. "Not great about the guard, but it's good we have a different guy to deal with."

Dedd was all business. I didn't sense he was going to try any crazy stuff, even though he was pulling on a pair of plastic surgical gloves. The more I was around him, the more it seemed he wasn't smart by any stretch of the imagination, but he was definitely as cunning as anyone I ever knew and relentless in his purpose as a shark with a snoot full of blood. Johnny Dedd seemed to be one of those rare guys you run into who possesses a total disregard for any potential consequence of his actions and a total commitment to his mission, even if the mission was vague, stupid, or had nothing to do with him. He'd jump into a fight, just because there was a fight. No *'higher purpose'* was required. I kind of admired that, as long as he trended towards the side of the *'good guys.'* And by *'good guys,'* I mean me.

I asked the obvious question, "How do you want to do this?"

"Give me a minute with the guard. I promise not to hurt him," Dedd answered.

"Go for it." I had no objections. I certainly wasn't going to wait all night to see if the guard left or fell asleep.

Dedd spoke to his cousin. "Pop the trunk, Joe."

Johnny hopped out of the car. He retrieved something from the trunk, then disappeared into the darkness with what looked like a ski mask in one hand and something metallic in the other. It seemed like he belonged in the shadows, too dangerous for daylight... like a vampire, or maybe something worse. It's difficult to define Johnny Dedd, which is good because that means people like him are few and far between.

Five minutes later, he returned and stuck his face in the passenger side window. "Grab your lock pick, Becker. Let's go."

We joined him and quick walked to the door.

We found Dedd had already choked out the guard, duct taped him up like a mummy, and wrote a bunch of anti-cop radical crap on the wall with spray paint. He tossed a wallet on the ground.

"What's that?" I asked.

"I picked a gang-banger's pocket after we left your office. He can have some fun trying to convince the cops he didn't do this shit." He waved his arm at his faux crime scene like the Wheel of Fortune lady introducing a puzzle.

My face must have given away my imagining the world of problems this might potentially cause.

"Don't worry. The guard," he pointed to the unconscious form on the ground, "will be bragging to the cops about how he fought off a half-dozen gang-banger radical terrorists before they took him down. Get your lock pick out and let's get this done."

I slid a short crowbar out of my interior jacket pocket and quickly sprung the lock.

"What the hell, Becker? I thought you said you had a lock-pick?" Tucker asked.

"Yeah, I do. It's called an Overtown Master Key... sorry to disappoint you, ladies."

Dedd chuckled. Tucker eye rolled. I went inside, the two beach boys following me like little baby ducklings following mother goose.

I directed Dedd to search the main floor while Tucker and I went back upstairs to re-toss the office.

It was good to bring in some fresh eyes. Tucker impressed me with his thorough and organized pattern-type search technique. I've never had the patience to do a search correctly when I was a cop... or after. I just used my instincts and my department issued cop-psychic-super-powers to find stuff, not unlike those guys who hold two bent sticks out in front of them and locate underground water in a cornfield. Once in a while, I'd take a shortcut and beat the location of various items out of somebody, but only if I knew for sure they were not a nice person. I never met very many nice people on the job, though. And now I'm well past the age of giving someone a well-deserved attitude adjustment... more or less.

Tucker actually carried out his search by the book while I reminisced and half-assed took another look around. I guess he is more disciplined than I am. He's definitely more disciplined than his cousin.

Respect.

There was a wooden chair beside one of the metal file cabinets. It didn't appear to be anything but a chair. Tucker saw it as a ladder. He pointed at the ceiling. "Becker, does that tile look ajar to you?"

Shit, it did. How did I miss that before?

"Yeah, it could be," I answered, like it wasn't a big deal.

I shouldn't have missed it before. Am I off my game? Are my best days behind me? Am I a has-been now?

Tucker hopped up on the chair and moved the loose tile. He had long arms. I hadn't noticed that earlier. He felt around the hole in the ceiling for a few seconds and then suddenly a nasty grin appeared on his face.

He found something.

"Becker, look at this."

Tucker showed me a black accounting ledger book. The chair was Schuster's step-stool he used to hide it in the ceiling.

Maybe these California pansies aren't so bad after all. Then Dedd walked in, sucking all the IQ points out of the room while munching on something.

"Hey, I found this box of candy bars on one of the shelves and it hasn't expired. I'm keeping them," he announced, as if anyone gave a shit.

"Did you find any evidence?" I asked, applying a thick coat of sarcasm that was lost on Johnny.

"No, just these snacks. Want one?"

Actually, a snack sounded pretty good. "Sure... your cousin found something."

Dedd handed me a candy bar. "He's good at finding stuff."

Tucker stayed focused. "This ledger refers to a smelter in Fresno, a small independent cargo airline in New Orleans, a small Atlantic based shipping company in Miami, and some entries about South Africa and Australia... some guy named Kruger shows up quite a few times. And the word Nauru appears several times too. I have no idea what this shit is, but I think it sounds like smugglers, Becker."

"Africa? Nauru? What the hell?" I was surprised. I never saw Schuster as anything more than a local fence. What would he be doing in international crime circles? This made little sense, unless something else was going on that was completely off our radar.

"Do you think they mean Krugerrand?" I asked.

"No, Kruger is a guy, or maybe a business name. I remember the krugerrand craze, but this isn't gold coins. There is another name here too... Komatski, Boris Komatski."

"Sounds Russian," Dedd said, allowing some discernible concern in his voice.

"I think it's polish," I replied. "My mother was polish... it's a common name."

Tucker elaborated. "This Komatski guy appears frequently in the ledger book. He's someone of significance."

I made a command decision, since I felt like I was in

command. "Let's get out of here. Tomorrow, we regroup and do a deep dive into the ledger."

Dedd spoke with a mouth full of candy, which I thought was rude. "Agreed,"

Tucker was still staring at the ledger pages, deep into the focused zone, but he heard me and responded. "Let's go." He tucked the book under his arm like a football.

I checked our guard on the way out. He was fine. I asked Tucker to go east for a couple of miles. I found a phone booth. Playing it cool, I had them park the car a block away from the phone booth. I kept my face concealed while I called 9-1-1- to get our security guard some help. These damned security and surveillance cameras are everywhere now. I even had to walk away in the wrong direction, then double back around the block.

These things used to be easier.

I miss easier.

Becker Residence - Lauderdale By The Sea

Morning came late, at least for me. I woke up with a slight headache. Sometimes that happens. I think it's caffeine withdrawal.

I pulled on some dark blue cotton shorts and a black v-neck t-shirt, wandered downstairs, and made a pot of coffee. I had a box of danish on the counter, so I took two of them, slapped a pad of butter on each one, plopped them on a plate, and tossed them into the microwave for thirty-seconds.

I brewed the pot of coffee using beans I ordered online from a small independent brand in Tucson. Apparently, the guy who roasts the beans was a retired cop. He roasts excellent coffee. I ordered some because it's called Filthy Pirate. I liked the name.

The paperback book I'd been reading was perched on the back of the couch where I last left it. I tucked the novel under my arm. I enjoy reading in the mornings, especially a Bronco Hammer literary masterpiece.

With a cup of coffee, a book, and some snacks in hand, I wandered out to the patio and took a moment to appreciate what was still good in life.

Being with the two sunshine boys on that job last night made me feel young again, at least for a little bit. It was a nice feeling.

But parking my butt in a waterfront Sifas luxury lounge chair with a nice cup of coffee made me feel comfortable and at peace. I wish I had someone to share it with. But I don't get along with anyone for very long. The standard was set too high before. I've become somewhat intolerant of others over these years of being alone. Or maybe, over time, people have just become obnoxious dicks who don't deserve my company... Or maybe I'm an obnoxious dick who doesn't have any friends. That would make more sense.

I noticed a couple of young kids walking along the edge of the water, trespassing the hell out of the condo docks. But they had fishing poles and grins. Who could complain? They weren't real trespassers; they were part of the local scene, the natural old-Florida way, from back when Anita Bryant still sold orange juice.

"Catching anything?" I asked the mandatory question that must be posed to all fishermen.

"Not yet, but we will," the taller of the two responded with the eternal optimism of youth. The kid was skinny, maybe ten years old, and wore the generic Florida kid uniform of denim shorts, tank top, and wide-brimmed straw hat... the littler of the two was maybe seven years old and dressed the same. They were obviously brothers with their matching freckles and scruffy blond hair.

I didn't engage further. I didn't need to. These were kids being kids and not bothering anyone. It was nice to see children not being rude little shits for a change.

I sipped coffee and relaxed. I had at least two or three hours before Frick and Frack would show up. It was obvious they weren't morning people.

I nibbled on my danish and took in some morning sun. My

mind drifted, but my thoughts kept coming back to the case. It wasn't like I was thinking about work; this was passion. I needed to know. Who whacked Schuster and why? Maybe if I could ditch the dynamic duo, I should go talk to the gold digger or whatever she was. Definitely, she was a loose end on this thing. And I needed to talk to my local connections. I can't let Harpo and Zeppo distract me.

And what about that ledger? I needed to get some of the pages photographed and sent to Dourdhoff Jenkins.

But the question I kept coming back to was why... Why did they torture Schuster? Why do I care? This whole case started with Schuster getting whacked. Then the mysterious note clouded up the water. Now we have a ledger, some big shot in California, and maybe a fraudulent gold bullion scheme... or was it all part of something else?

Hopefully, we would see a breakthrough in the case today... and then what? The Los Angeles Laurel and Hardy show would be gone... not that I'd miss them, but once Dedd and Tucker left, I'd have nothing interesting going on... I should enjoy this case while it's happening. No sense rushing it. Sometimes you have to stop and smell the roses, even if said roses are fraud, murder, and torture.

The two kids I saw wandered out of sight further down the docks on their way to a better fishing spot.

I went inside for a coffee refill. This time I bought a thermos full out with me, a bottle of Jack, and my case file. Might as well read some more. Maybe I'd get a bright idea.

I flicked an ash off my cigarette into my Tommy Bahama ashtray and freshened up my coffee cup with some hot black Tucson brew with a splash of whiskey for medicinal purposes. I might have felt a chill earlier. Why take chances?

The Offices Of Becker Investigations

My California guests, private detectives Abbott and Costello, showed up just before eleven in the morning. They both displayed obvious hangover symptoms. At that age, I would've had the same too if I was working a case out of town... or in town. Which is the thing about places like Florida and California. They always seem like everyone is on a permanent vacation.

"Nice digs, Becker," Tucker offered as he followed me through the condo from the front door to the patio.

"I've been thrown out of worse joints," Dedd added.

"I might throw you out of this joint if either of you drunk bastards puke on my boat dock."

"I'm good. No worries," Tucker assured me, although not convincingly.

"Do you two want some coffee? I have some danish too."

"I could eat," Dedd replied, accepting my offer.

"Tucker?"

"Sure... just coffee, though. I have some kind of tropical flu bug I think."

"Like too many mojitos?"

"Perhaps... Mojitos are no longer my favorite drink. After about twenty of them, they start to taste weird."

We gathered around a patio table to compare notes and theories. We had a pretty good stack of documents already. Tucker tossed the ledger into the middle of pile.

"So what next?" I asked.

"Do you have a mirror? I feel like my hair is messed up." Deddario said.

"Yeah, in the hallway on the right."

"Thanks."

He disappeared back inside.

I knew Dedd wouldn't be much help for planning and analysis work, so I went ahead started the discussion with his cousin rather than waiting. "Tucker?"

He pursed his lips in thought, then spoke. "It's dense... and from what I can figure out, it's big. Maybe bigger than we thought."

"Like what?" I asked.

"I'll explain when my vain cousin finishes staring at himself in the mirror."

"A mirror? Like a parakeet?" I snorted.

Tucker snorted back. "Yeah, except a parakeet has a bigger brain."

Johnny wandered back in and joined us.

"Like I was saying, Becker. I read through this ledger last night and found some strange shit. Most of it has the stench of smuggling and fraud on it."

"For example?"

"Looks like you were right. Kruger isn't a dude... Kruger might, emphasis on might, be referencing a lost gold stash in Africa."

"No shit?"

"Yes shit. And it gets worse. Nauru isn't a guy either, it's a place... some rogue island full of criminals and money launderers off the coast of Australia. It's home to some real bad actors."

"Not good."

"Exactly."

"So, what does it all mean?"

"I'd like to send a copy of the ledger to Mister Stump. He's good with numbers and analytics."

"I think I spoke to Stump on the phone. An... interesting gentlemen," I said, choosing my words carefully.

"No, he's not interesting. He's a nasty old asshole, but he's our asshole and he's damned good with numbers and details. He might find the transactions that led to Schuster's death and our client's financial loss."

"That makes sense. Do it. What else?"

Tucker continued, "Next we need to find some background

on the shipping company that is mentioned in the ledger... that's a local lead, or at least the company has vessels that dock in South Florida... someplace in Miami... somehow the shipping firm is tied to a guy named Boris Komatski."

"Interesting. Never heard of him. But I'm guessing we're talking about the Port of Miami if they are commercial vessels."

"Yeah. It looks like there is shipping going from various ports in Africa, Nauru, and Florida. We'll need to dig into all this some more. It might explain a lot for both of us. Did you have anything new?"

"I might have another lead," I added. It seemed like the right time to disclose the gold digger. "Schuster was dating a woman. She might have set him up."

"Let me handle that," Johnny suggested, finally joining in the discussion. "Women love me. It's a curse and a gift," he explained.

"Fine with me," I said. "I'll write down the details and give them to you. The more I consider her possible involvement, it might be a good idea for me to stay off her radar as long as possible. "

I was caught up in the synergy of our brainstorming session. These two guys might be pathetic and disgusting losers, but they were good at their job. I suddenly realized I was enjoying myself... and around people too, which is unusual... if you can call these two feckless turds people.

Tucker offered up another idea. "We have a woman in our office, Joan Vance, who is a top tier organized crime expert. I'm going to ask her to look at our client to see what it is he isn't telling us."

"Do you trust her on something like this?" I asked, for no reason really. I just wanted to see how he reacted.

"Of course I trust her. We're engaged."

Tucker puffed up a bit as he spoke. I must have pushed one of his buttons.

Dedd laughed out loud, "No, you're not... quit telling people that, Joe. If Joan hears about you spreading that shit, she will beat your skinny ass senseless."

That response seemed to let some of the air out of Tucker's sails.

"Fine," he said, somewhat dejectedly. "We *have* dated in the past, though. But I *do* trust her. Joan went out on a medical retirement from Beverly Hills PD. She was gut shot in an ambush at the Los Angeles Harbor. She's hard-core."

"Gut shot? Is she up for a job like this?" I asked, again looking more for a reaction than an answer.

"She's fine," he insisted. "They just processed her out of the police department with a fat pension and payout."

"How did she score that?"

"After we wrapped that case where she got shot, she had so much dirt on the Southern California political elite that they would have had to make her mayor of L.A. if she asked them.

"Nice." I was impressed with her actually shaking up the powers that be. Who knew there was rampant corruption in Los Angeles... besides everybody?

"So, what do we do today?" Johnny asked as he ambled back into the kitchen for another cup of coffee. He was clearly more of a doer than a thinker.

"Johnny, you check out the local gold digger woman. Tucker, you send the file to Stump. I'll talk to some cop buddies. I should hear something about Schuster's autopsy today. Then I might take a drive down to Miami late this afternoon and shoot some pictures around the shipping company, see if I can pick up anything on this Komatski guy."

Tucker nodded enthusiastically, "Let me know before you go down there. I'd like to ride along if you don't care."

"Sounds good." I said. "If you can get someone in your shop to check out the possibility of Schuster having an adult daughter in California, that will help too. It's thin, she might not exist. So I'd make it a back burner issue."

"So, can we hang out here and drink coffee for a while? I kind of like this place," Johnny said as he got comfortable in a lounger.

"Make yourselves at home. I am going to go shower and dress. Make your calls, do what you need to do. I have a spare key I'll loan you."

Dedd gave me a thumbs up. "Cool... You know Becker, for an old fart, you aren't bad."

I might have felt the twitch of a grin in the corner of my mouth at that left-handed compliment. Probably not, though.

"Don't make me beat your ass, Johnny. I might be old, but I fight dirty and a life sentence is meaningless to me."

"I wouldn't have it any other way, sir."

I gave him the finger.

He laughed.

I laughed.

It was time to shower and get ready for the day. I think we will get some traction now. Good times.

On The Road To Miami

Other than a day of making calls and shuffling paper, Tucker and I didn't accomplish much. That's how cases go sometimes... nothing, nothing, then everything... you just have to keep pressing until something breaks.

Tucker sat back quietly in the passenger seat of the Jaguar, enjoying the drive down the coast to the Port of Miami even though we got a late start. We wouldn't get there until after sunset, but that was fine. This mission was just a quick recon.

Tucker broke the silence with a question. "Did you get any feedback on the autopsy, Becker?"

"Yeah, not much help. He was tortured for a couple of hours, then took one to the back of the head. It was professionals. I think they got what they wanted or else they decided he didn't give up some information they didn't want getting out... either way, it was not a good day to be Mister Schuster."

"Tough break. But if he was an asshole, he had to know things would eventually turn to shit on him. It always does."

"Not always… but most of the time."

"Yeah."

It was my turn to ask a question or two. "Did you hear anything from Stump yet? Or your organized crime girl?"

"Stump is still working on it. He's one of those guys you don't bug about things. He just gets it done and tells you… Joan will call tonight with an update on our client. Which reminds me, Deb sent a memorandum of understanding for you to sign. It clears you as a professional services partner so we can legally give you all the information on our client. You can do a digital signature on your phone."

"No, I don't do digital shit. I'll print it and sign it and give it to you back at my place or the office."

"Why don't you do digital?" Tucker asked.

"Because I'm an American."

"Oh."

"I don't do metric either."

"Funny."

"No, it's not." Tucker was starting to piss me off.

"I mean funny like a coincidence… or something… not 'haha' funny. Stump told me the same thing once."

"Wise man." I changed the subject. "The exit for the harbor is next. We're looking for a shed just off Port Boulevard. If we are lucky, their one registered vessel that we know of will be in port, the Tyvehule, Danish registry."

"Got it… Tyvehule."

Ten minutes later, I talked our way through security with my phony court order. We were cruising along at about five miles an hour looking for something.

Tucker whispered, "There it is, the Tyvehule. Two o'clock."

To his credit, he didn't point or physically react in any way that anyone who might see us would notice, definitely the subtle reaction of a professional.

I drove down to a public parking area a few of hundred yards past the vessel and pulled into a spot between a couple of trucks. I popped the trunk and retrieved a set of night vision goggles, a camera, and my blackjack, just in case.

Tucker quietly exited the car and joined me.

It was dark out now. I wasn't sure yet how far I'd go with this, so our impromptu operation was definitely a tune played by ear.

Tucker tapped my shoulder and signaled he wanted to whisper something in my ear. I stopped and nodded.

"Stay in the shadows and let me talk to anyone we find outside the boat. This stuff is kind of my thing."

I gave him a nod and found a place to duck into the darkness and disappear while he worked his magic.

I watched Tucker approach a man who might have been a guard for the Tyvehule. Tucker casually offered the guy a smoke, then did some Dice Clay moves with a cigarette lighter. I couldn't hear all of what was being said, but the man got chatty right away.

I know there were some words that sounded like, 'hey I'm the new guy for this other boat 'and something about 'we're bringing in a shipment of rum. 'Then some real chatter started.

I started watching through my night vision goggles and almost chuckled out loud when the guy pulled out a piece of paper, wrote something down, and handed it to Tucker.

There were some more words exchanged, then the guy hugged Tucker, and they both exchanged waves as he walked off.

I snapped a couple of photos, chilled for a few minutes, then met Tucker back at the Jag.

"What in the hell did you tell that guy?" I asked with more than a hint of amusement and admiration in my voice.

"It's a gift. I told him I was a new guy, gave him a cigarette, and chatted him up. I'm good at icebreakers."

"What did you do, take a Carnegie course?"

"Who?"

"Never mind."

"It's no big deal, Becker. It's just what I do. But he had plenty to say."

"Like what?"

"Like he's been working on that boat for four years. Their shipping company was bought out by some shady corporation in Nauru, and he thinks they have been smuggling something valuable back and forth from Africa for the past year... something heavy. They just offloaded a shipment into some trucks this morning. They leave again in three days after taking on some cargo for a French company."

"He told you all that shit over a cigarette?"

"I told him I could score them a couple of cases of rum before they left. That helped."

"Wow."

"Something else... he said they installed additional bunks on board. Enough for about fifty men... and the crew requirements for this vessel are only a dozen guys."

"You really *did* chat this guy up," I commented. But Tucker wasn't done.

"Then he told me he had a sister who would like to meet me. But if she looks like him, well, it might not be worth the risk. That whole unibrow and thick beard thing isn't attractive on a woman."

"You are one charming son of a bitch, Tucker..."

"Thank you."

"But why do I not like you, then? It doesn't add up. I like everybody."

"I got a feeling that you might be exaggerating, Becker. I don't think you like anybody."

"Well, you might be right, kid. Let's go see what your cousin found out.

Becker Residence - Lauderdale By The Sea

We each had a drink and a plate of snacks in front of us

as we picked away at the huge tray of hors d'oeuvres centered on the table that I ordered from the Tiki Club Restaurant two blocks down the street. This is dockside dining at its best at Chez Becker.

I'd already printed, signed, and emailed a photographed copy of the memorandum of understanding back, so I suppose now I'm officially part of the Tucker Investigations team. I've joined worse outfits. I just can't remember when.

It was getting late, maybe midnight, and Dedd had only shown up about twenty minutes before. He was limping a little and was uncharacteristically disheveled, as if he had been in a serious traffic accident. He'd also had a bit too much to drink. Not that Tucker and I hadn't. We'd been hitting the liquor cabinet pretty hard since we got back from Miami.

Johnny Dedd was unusually reserved.

"So what happened, Johnny? Did you get to talk to the woman?" I asked.

"Uh… yes."

"And did she say anything?" I asked again, feeling like this was going to be more like a cross-examination with a hostile witness instead of a conversation.

"Not much."

"What the hell is wrong with you Dedd?" I asked the glassy-eyed Romeo from California.

"Uh… she was a little more than I expected, Becker… I think I threw my back out and sprained my wrist. My nose hurts again too."

"But did you get any information, mister seduction?" Tucker asked, only half-amused at his cousin's condition.

"I found out that just because a woman is past fifty, doesn't mean she can't hurt you… she knows things, Joe," he said with eyes like a man who has seen too much combat. "She knows things I've never even heard of."

"But did she tell you anything?" I asked of our shell-shocked Casanova, this time a bit more forcefully.

"No, but in my defense, I didn't tell her anything either."

"Well, that's something, I guess," I said, accepting that his mission was a gigantic waste of time.

"But I *did* find out where she lives, what kind of car she has, and what color her bathroom towels are... come on guys, I've been used and abused in the name of justice... You could lighten up a little."

Was Johnny Dedd whining? Yeah, I think Johnny Dedd is whining.

"So the famous Johnny Dedd got spanked by an older woman," Tucker said loudly with a huge grin.

Dedd was still in his defensive mode. "There was no spanking, Joe... but some of that other stuff... Holy crap."

"So Tucker and I can still run surveillance on her. At least that's something," I groused.

"I put a tracker on her car and one in her purse, so that might help," Dedd disclosed.

It's like pulling teeth with this guy. We asked if she gave up information, which he answered, but we didn't ask if he took any other investigative action. You definitely have to be specific with Dedd. I better remember that next time. If I don't strangle him first.

"That definitely helps, Johnny," Tucker said, demonstrating more patience with his psycho cousin than I could provide. I think Joe was trying to spare any more damage to Dedd's very sensitive ego.

Johnny asked us a question next. It was unclear if he was truly curious or if he just wanted the spotlight off his steamy little investigative liaison." What did you guys find out at the harbor?"

"It looks like we are on the right track. Everything is tied into the theory that this involves some kind of international smuggling ring," Tucker replied.

"Any word from Joan?" Dedd asked.

Tucker looked a bit dismayed. "Not yet. She'll probably call tomorrow."

I looked at my watch. It wasn't that late in L.A. "Call her."

"She'll call," Tucker said while he avoided making eye contact.

"Why don't you want to call her?" I pressed.

"Because I don't want to look desperate," he finally confessed.

"You puss," I growled, having no patience with a lovelorn dolt.

Dedd joined in now, gleeful at seeing someone else in the tribe taking heat instead of him." You *are* a puss... She's probably on a date. You know that, don't you?"

I sensed that comment would leave a mark.

"She's not seeing anyone. She would have told me."

"You make me puke," Dedd proclaimed a bit aggressively than the situation called for.

"You make me puke," Tucker countered, obviously not the world's greatest debater.

Then Dedd took a half-hearted swing at Tucker, which missed. Tucker lumbered into him and countered with an elbow. It also missed.

I jumped up, grabbed both of them in a hair-connect lock, one of the most painful compliance holds ever created by nuns, and pulled them in close.

"NOT IN MY HOUSE, IDIOTS!"

"Sorry, Becker," Tucker said.

They immediately calmed down, so I almost let them go. But then... Dedd had to be an ass. "Yeah, Becker. My cousin's a dick. I apologize for him too."

Tucker redlined again. "*You're* a dick!" He attempted another drunk swing.

The dispute escalated back up into the unacceptable behavior zone. I cranked down my grip on their hair, demanded they empty their pockets of guns and tech onto the table, which they did on their tip toes amid of yelps of pain, then I marched them over to the canal and pushed them both in.

I went back to my drink.

As meetings go, this wasn't the best... but it wasn't the worst either. Nobody got shot. Yet.

A much more wet and subdued Dedd and Tucker crawled back up on the dock and returned silently to their drinks.

"Sorry, Becker."

"Sorry, Becker."

"Forget it... it seems like Joan Vance is a touchy subject. Give me her number. I'll call her tomorrow if she doesn't call tonight. Capisce?"

"Got it."

"Works for me."

"Good... Now you drunk assholes call a ride-share and go back to your hotel. I don't want to see your sorry asses for the next twelve hours."

"Fair enough, Becker."

"Sorry, Becker, it won't happen again."

"It might happen again, but next time I'm using my blackjack," I threatened.

"Got it."

They wandered out of the house and I finally had peace and quiet again.

I lit a cigarette, picked up my drink, and walked over to the edge of the canal.

Tranquility... a pleasant drink... beautiful evening lights dancing over the water as the tide went back out to the sea.

But I already missed having those two worthless morons around.

I missed police work.

I missed a lot of things.

Life is complicated.

CHAPTER 5

At around nine in the morning Florida time, I called retired Beverly Hills PD and ex-LA County Organized Crime Task Force Detective Lieutenant Joan Vance at the Tucker Investigations California business number. I didn't know what to expect. I was pleasantly surprised.

"This is Joan Vance." Curt, professional, to the point.

I liked it.

"This is Becker from Fort Lauderdale. I believe your organization received my signed memorandum last night."

"Yes, Mister Becker. We're all good now as far as information sharing. I've read up on you a little. It's nice to be working with a professional."

"You are too kind, Lieutenant Vance."

"Joan is fine."

"Becker is fine for me."

She responded with a charming little chuckle. "Well, Becker… it looks like we stepped in some shit with our client."

"How so?"

"The man who hired us is trying desperately to un-hire us. It seems he was firmly leaned upon."

"How so?"

"Our guy is named Dagmaier Dubois. He's a Los Angeles socialite with a hefty trust fund, a local fine arts contributor, and he has a very hidden stake in our local professional basketball team."

"Sounds like a pillar of society."

"Except for the part about him occasionally moving some stolen fine art. And recently, getting a bunch of investors together to buy into a lost treasure scam. Dubois was duped into investing heavily in the lost Kruger gold. Turns out there were a few bricks of gold used as a flash and the other ton and a half were painted bricks."

"Ouch... How much is 'invested heavily?" I asked.

"He told us thirteen million. But today I found out it was something closer to the tune of forty-million dollars. About half of Hollywood and a sizable chunk of Malibu and the Santa Monica elite invested with him."

"That's not good."

"It gets worse."

"I can't wait to hear this," I said.

"One of the investors is Russian mob connected. A guy named Igor Kuznetsov. They say he's the lone Russian survivor of Eagle Rock."

"Eagle Rock? I thought that was some crazy fairy tale. One guy against four hundred Russian gangsters. It really happened?"

"I think there was more than one guy. We probably shouldn't discuss it over the phone... I said more than I should, so you would know I was serious."

"I'm sorry I know this information," I said in all sincerity for the benefit of any secret organization which might be monitoring this call.

Joan continued, "So, fast forwarding to the end, our client wants to get the money back, pay back the investors, get the scam shut down, and make the whole shit show go away."

"I want world peace and free beer for life, but it ain't gonna happen. I think you should prepare your client for disappointment."

She ignored my warning and continued. "More good news. Rumor has it that Igor is heading for the Miami area. His mood is, let's just say, irritable. If he can't get to our guy, he'll be going to the source."

"What a swell guy." I said with a big sloppy serving of

sarcasm. "Just what we needed."

"Tell me about it... the only name he has is Schuster. So, with Schuster dead, he's going to be working his way up the food chain."

"Fun."

"Yeah, good times. When he got word that we were looking into it, he threatened to whack our client, which wouldn't break my heart except we won't get paid. So, our boy Dagmaier heard about the threats and is threatening to fire us. He's not what I would describe as 'thinking clearly 'right now, Becker."

"When they get to the point of needing a private investigator, they never think clearly."

Joan agreed. "Very true, Becker."

"So what about this Boris guy from the ledger? Did anyone find anything on him or his shipping company yet?"

"Only bad news. He's an international asshole who is suspected of human trafficking, fraud, and aiding and abetting terrorists. We don't know much more than that about him yet. A lot of his file seems to be locked down by the feds. I think they want him, but my guess is Boris is too smart for them. So it might be up to us to bag this piece of shit... or at least if we were all still cops, it would be on us. I'm not fully used to the private sector yet, Becker," Joan admitted. "It's a different ball game."

"Same ball game, Joan. We just play short stop now instead of pitching. But taking down Boris isn't off the table if it comes to that. I'm hoping we can find the money and clear up Schuster's murder."

"That would be nice. It sounds like we're heading in the right direction."

"What are you doing on your end, Joan?"

"Mister Stump and Mister Coulter, two of our associates in the agency, are providing around the clock protection. They have him hidden locally. So DuBois is fine... he doesn't realize it, but he's probably the safest he's ever been in his life with those two guarding him... and if he mentions terminating the contract again, Mister Stump will rip his lips off and make him kiss his own ass."

"I talked to Mister Stump. He's sounds quite competent. Is Coulter any good?"

"Coulter is the best. He's a disciplined top tier military contractor who went to work with us after a little mess with some local politicians we got involved in. He's good."

"Sounds like he's a 'what's wrong with this picture' puzzle alongside Tucker and Dedd."

"They all get along pretty good, surprisingly."

"All right. Sounds like you are on top of it. What can we do to help on this end?" I asked.

"If you find Boris, point Johnny at him and yell 'sic em' and then call the coroner with an estimated body count. Otherwise, just find the money and avoid Igor. He will give you a bit of trouble."

"If there is a fight looming, Johnny Dedd will probably find it."

That elicited a chuckle from her.

"So, how are you getting along with the boys, Becker?" she asked.

"Actually, I'm having a little bit of fun working with them. So far, I only had to kick their asses once."

"Oh, details please," she giggled. It was a very sexy giggle. I can see why she has Tucker so pizzle-sprung.

"They got drunk and mouthed off, so I had to toss them in a canal to cool them down. But we're good now."

"I'd give a million bucks to have seen that... I was afraid without Mister Stump there, they would get in trouble. I'm glad you are aboard, Becker. Call me if you need anything."

"Copy that. Nice talking to you, Joan. Call me likewise if I can help." Then I remembered something. "Joan, before we go, the guys were supposed to ask about a possible daughter for Schuster. She is an adult living in California, if she exists at all."

"Yeah, we have nothing so far. Still checking."

"One last thing, Joan. If you run across anything about someone named Grande or Pas... let me know. I don't know if they are Mexican nationals, or a nickname, or just a local surname... I have no idea what they might have to do with this."

"I'll keep an ear to the ground."

"Sounds good. Thanks again. Talk to you later."

We disconnected.

I like her. She's definitely too good for Tucker.

I left my building and walked over to the beach diner on Commerce where I ordered some eggs over easy and a double side of home fried potatoes... Being pleasant makes me hungry. By one in the afternoon, I was back behind my desk sipping coffee and reading notes.

I had Pancho and Lefty meet me at the office after lunch. I had no intention of letting them back in my house until I knew their heads were back on straight.

Tucker came in first with Dedd walking sheepishly behind him.

"Sit down, butt holes," I commanded.

They sat.

"No more bullshit?" I asked.

"No, we're done," Tucker said, the smarter of the two speaking for the pair.

"Good. This case just got interesting." I relayed my conversation with Joan and summarized everything we did, found out, or discovered from the beginning.

"So we go after Boris?" Dedd asked.

"Yes. We go after Boris."

"Where can we find him?"

"I have a feeling Johnny's date from last night might know where he is. Anyone up for a three car surveillance?"

Johnny appeared nervous. "We're just following, right? I don't have to make contact again?"

"No... just following right now."

"Cool."

I gave Johnny the keys to an old Ford Taurus 'beater car' I picked up at a police auction. I store in the office parking garage for exactly this purpose. I call it a 'context' car. If you are acting like a cop, it looks like a believable cop car. If you are presenting yourself as a middle-class guy, it passes as the second family car. If you are pretending to be a dirt bag, it look like a dirt bag set of wheels. Depending on the context you provide, it is convincing in almost any situation you need it for.

Tucker took the rental car, and I drove the Jag. With the tracking device, a three car tail would work. Usually in a city, we would prefer to have seven cars, but with technology we could pull it off with three and not get spotted. We could fit into almost any neighborhood with at least one of the cars. The funny thing is, you can drive a beater into the nicest neighborhood in town and no one will think much of it, but taking a Jaguar into the hood meant there would be eyes on you, because you're either an apex predator or a mark. The Taurus looked a lot like an old city detective car because it was an old city detective car. But there are so many of that model on the road, if you act right, no one will pick up on you.

An hour later, we were in position around her condo. With technical tracking and top of the line communication tools, we were set.

We had Tucker take the eye on her digs. She hadn't seen him before and he wouldn't draw much attention.

The purse transponder showed she was in her home. I figured she wouldn't leave before happy hour and, as usual, I was correct.

At around four, the garage door opened, and she backed out onto the street.

Tucker called it, "Target moving."

I took point as she came down the street, calling the tail for the other two cars.

We code named her Goldie... no sense saying her name on

radio in the off chance that might be intercepted, no matter how unlikely that was.

Goldie drove south, taking us into Dade County. She used surface streets. She stopped at a drugstore. She drove to a bar in an upscale neighborhood and stayed for about an hour. Then lady luck was with us. She drove South toward the Port of Miami. Anywhere in that area sounded like a good place to find Boris.

It was dark enough now for Johnny to take the point. With a ball cap and fake glasses, he wouldn't be as easy to spot, unless she keyed in on that bent beak of his.

"She's moving past the Port of Miami turn off... I think she's going further south... stand by... confirmed continuing south," Johnny announced.

I gave an order, "Tucker, take point. Johnny, fall in behind me."

"Copy that."

"Moving."

Tucker began calling it. "Continuing south."

"Where in the hell is she going?" Dedd asked.

"Destination unknown... did you guys remember to bring guns and extra ammo?"

"Uh... no... we're traveling light. Why? Do we need guns and extra ammo?"

"If she gets on the freeway again and heads to the Keys... we will be in for a possible shit show... because when bad guys go to the Keys, they get their inner pirate on. And it ain't pretty."

"No shit."

"No shit, Johnny. Don't worry. I have extra equipment packed in the Jag and Taurus. I've been down this path before."

"Cool... this violence stuff is all new to me. I'm a lover, not a fighter."

"Your history says otherwise."

"All that stuff was overblown."

"No, dumbass. I'm talking about your run-in with the gold

digger. That old cougar kicked your ass. That doesn't say much to support the 'Johnny Dedd Love Machine' reputation."

There was a long silence... then...

"This is Dedd... my radio seems to be malfunctioning... I'll be..."

Tucker cut him off. "She's doubling back on us. This looks like a heat run. Target is heading North."

I couldn't believe it. I don't think she made us, so Tucker was probably right. It was a heat run, a tactic drug dealers occasionally do to draw out surveillance. It's just a random drive with a few screwy maneuvers thrown in to trip up any inexperienced detectives and then head home again. I've seen them do it ten times a night when I was a cop, depending on how coked up they were.

A young detective might call this a bad break. An old detective knows this is 'confirmation.' If we were on the job, we could use this observation in a wiretap affidavit. But we are private detectives, or as most people refer to us, borderline assholes. So getting legal documents before a judge is the least of our worries. We knew Goldie was up to some shit, and because she made a run to particular spots of interest to us, I believe this confirmed she was a legitimate target in the investigation of Schuster's death. I just hoped we didn't wind up in the Keys before this case was over... That would be bad. We would be operating behind enemy lines. Because other than the tourists and fishermen, there are a lot of assholes down there in the Conch Republic.

I decided we needed to call it a night and regroup tomorrow. I made the official announcement. "Head home boys, we pick this back up in the morning. She's playing games tonight. Make it ten-thirty mañana."

"Copy that."

"Copy that."

I needed a drink, and I was long overdue to speak with a local contact. There was a beach bar on the Pier in Lauderdale by the Sea run by a guy named Thom. I needed to bend Thom's ear for some local knowledge, general intelligence gathering, and to enjoy an ice cold post-surveillance beer. Thom was a large man from Long Island, New York. He knew everything and everybody in town. If I *had* a friend in town, which I didn't, it might be Thom.

I took a stool at the small winding bar. Thom spotted me and grabbed two beers. He knew me well enough to know that one bottle wouldn't get the job done. I knew him well enough to know I wouldn't be drinking alone.

"What's up, Becker?" he asked as he parked himself on the stool beside me. He surreptitiously poured half of my second beer in a plastic cup and quickly slammed in down in one gulp, hoping no one from the liquor board saw him.

The big man was the typical old-school Long Island transplant, not one of these new commie pukes we get now. He got sick of the city, switched his party affiliation to Republican, pulled on a size 4x Hawaiian shirt and bought a beach bar in Florida, while, of course, maintaining his accent. Like any big man, he was huffing and puffing as he had been scrambling for hours, which he had. Thom ran a tight ship.

"I'm working a job," I told him. "Do you remember Schuster?"

"The fence?"

"Yeah."

"Dead, right?"

"Like a doornail."

"Good," he grunted as he picked up a big glass of water and chugged it. He set the glass back down and wiped his mouth with the back of his forearm. "I get thirsty when I work," he explained for no reason.

I didn't care that he was thirsty. I wanted to know what happened between him and Schuster. "Bad blood between you two?" I asked.

"Just normal."

"How so?"

"He came in here drunk, loud, and running his mouth about

some California deal he was in that was going to make him millions, which is fine, but then he hit on some tourist's wife, who was totally hot..."

"Big boobs?"

"Yeah."

"Makes sense. He was a boob man... so then what happened?"

"This particular tourist wasn't a slouch, though. He drives a cab in Vegas for a living..."

"Psychopath?"

"Probably." Thom shrugged at my logical conclusion.

"So then what happened?"

"The tourist shoves Schuster and tells him to back the fuck off."

"And?"

"And of course, mister 'shit for brains 'Schuster pulls a gun... I mean, he was drunk as shit, Becker."

"Big mistake." I didn't recall ever seeing Schuster that drunk... this seemed odd. He was a sneaky shit too, so public bragging didn't add up either. He did religiously pack a Roscoe though, so that part was consistent with the Schuster I knew.

Thom got my mind back on track as he continued his story. "Yeah. So, I told you I played some minor league ball, right?"

"About a million times."

"Well, I did... anyway, I was too far away from the action to directly intervene, so I threw a bottle of Butt Whisker beer at him. It was probably clocking about seventy miles an hour when it beaned him."

"Knock his ass out?"

"Oh hell yeah, knocked his ass the fuck out."

"Damn. Shame to waste a good Butt Whisker," I commented, somewhat accusingly.

"It's what I had in my hand." he said apologetically, with a face full of guilt and regret.

"Exigent circumstances."

"Huh?"

"Cop term."

"Oh… good to know. So, I have a couple of the bus boys drag his unconscious ass out to his car and drive him over to a safe place to sleep it off.."

"How did that work out?"

"Fine, until the cops arrested him for being drunk behind the wheel in the police parking lot."

"So, what's the bad blood part of this?"

"Oh yeah, so about a week later, me and him was having coffee and the son of a bitch stiffed me on a deal."

"How so?"

"The sleazy bastard showed me a photo of a nice Rolex Yacht-Master II he had in his safe, absolutely guaranteed to be probably not stolen. He asked if I wanted to buy it for ten grand, which is a smoking deal, you know that."

"Sounds stolen."

"Totally not stolen, Becker. I think Schuster respected me enough not to lie about something like that."

"You just knocked his ass out the week before."

"Yeah, but that was business."

"Fine… not stolen… So what happened?"

"He needed some quick cash. So, I gave him five grand down and then never saw him again. Maybe because he got whacked, so… no hard feelings, I guess.

"Yeah, being dead constitutes a reasonable excuse, I suppose."

"I know, right? So, Becker, will you look into that for me too? I'll give you five hundred bucks if you get the watch *or* my money for me."

"I'll keep an eye out, big man. You never know how these things will turn out."

"Nice."

He seemed happy at the prospects of getting his money back, as slim as those prospects were.

"Did he say *why* he needed quick cash?" I asked.

"No... but he seemed a little desperate. He low-balled it right out of the chute... that ain't like him."

I wasn't getting anything concrete from this line of discussion, so I decided to dig into some associates. "Ever see him with anybody, Thom?"

"Other than the gold digger?"

"Gold digger? Who, Jeanine Faraday? The crazy woman?" I asked, surprised he mentioned the woman we'd been following.

"Yeah, you know her?" Thom asked.

"Reputation only."

Thom elaborated. "We call her the horny gold digger. She might be crazy too. I don't know." Thom said quite solemnly, as if he were delivering bad news.

"Yeah, it sounds like we're talking about the same tomato. What do you know about her?"

"Not much. She drifted into town about a year ago from Los Angeles. She always dresses to the nines like she's heading for a nightclub. I understand she scored some big cash scamming and seducing a few of the old retired rich guys around here, got herself a nice condo, a nice car, lots of jewelry... I think that's how she knew Schuster. He sold the jewelry for her and replaced it with quality fakes so her suitors wouldn't know the difference. Her and Schuster were almost like business partners. Then something happened, and she went back to LA for a few weeks about a month ago."

"How do you know so much about her?"

"Some of the old guys she ripped off come in here for happy hour. They keep tabs on her."

"Oh, are they pissed off?"

"Not really. Most of them think it was worth it." His eyes darted side to side like a lizard as he lowered his voice. "According to what they tell me, she knows things, Becker... forbidden things, if you get my drift."

"I'd rather not."

"No shit." He snorted at my comment. "It's best we don't know, Becker, it's for the best." The wisdom of a beach bar manager is equal to, or greater than, any of those mystical swamis or fortune tellers you read about.

"So is she back now?" I asked, not letting on what I already knew, not because I didn't trust Thom, but because a competent investigator knows when and how to compartmentalize information. Thom tells me stuff because I got him out of some shit back when I was a cop and he was a young dumbass. It was one of those wrong place-wrong time deals that could have wound him up in prison, even though he doesn't have more than one or two dishonest bones in his body. We became friends. Plus, he runs a bar, so he's special. He doesn't spread around any details of our private chats to others. He's discreet for a friendly guy, and he's an excellent judge of character. If he ever left the hospitality field, I'd hire him on the spot for my agency.

Thom answered my question. "She's back, and she's up to some shit. I spotted her over there."

He pointed to his upscale competitor across the street. It was ten times nicer and twelve times more expensive than Thom's joint.

He continued, "She was in a corner booth with some mobbed up clown. He wasn't from around here and he wasn't a tourist. They were talking shop rather than her mastery of the perverse arts, if you get my meaning."

I thought for him not being a fan of hers, he seems to bring up her special talents quite often.

"Any idea who the guy was?"

"Funny you should ask. One of the codgers she scammed was in the place too. He tipped a waitress a hundred bucks to find out. He told me it was some big time pro-sports owner guy out of Los Angeles. I got to tell you, Becker, he looked like a total puss."

"Total puss?" I asked, not completely sure how he was using that term.

"Exactly... a total puss."

"Name?" I tried to maintain my normal facial expression of polite but detached listening. It was difficult. This could be a break.

"Yeah, he got a name, but I forget... it was something stupid... French maybe? Something about a sandwich."

"Dagmaier Dubois?"

"Shit... yeah... that's it.. I was thinking Dagwood." Thom said.

"Dagwood? That's a very old school sandwich, Thom."

For some reason, any mention of historic sandwiches always takes precedent over business with me, and evidently Thom feels the same way. Sandwiches are delicious.

"Yes, the Dagwood is old school, but still epic," Thom explained as he stared wistfully over the ocean, probably imagining a giant sandwich floating in the sky out there.

"So, it was definitely Dubois?" I asked, forcing myself to get back on track before I followed Thom to fantasy sandwich land.

"Yeah, that's the name."

"Did Schuster have any other 'inner-circle 'types?"

"Just Bogan."

"Who?" I asked.

"He's a goon. Australian guy... He's new. Bogan ran the warehouse and did leg breaking or whatever it was you used to do for Schuster before you guys had that falling out."

"I wasn't a leg breaker... just an intimidator. I hardly ever hurt anybody very much unless they were a jerk." Hearing myself described as a leg breaking was unnerving and a bit insulting. But I'm used to insults... so... no big deal, I guess.

Thom elaborated, "I remember when you was a cop, you put a lot of guys in the hospital, Becker. People are still afraid of you."

"Good. They should be. But I'm just an old man now. There is nothing dangerous about me anymore." I felt a little pity party starting in my head. I pushed it aside. "So tell me about Bogan."

"Big slob, tall, maybe three hundred pounds, used to be a professional wrestler in Australia."

"They have professional wrestling in Australia?" I asked.

"Sure. Why wouldn't they?"

"Because their country is crawling with monsters and giant bugs. I'd think they fight just to stay alive every day. How would they have time to watch wrestling?"

"What the hell do you know about Australia, Becker?"

"All their TV shows and movies are about crocodiles or someone named crocodile. Also, I remember they had that song about the land down under. I don't care for crocodiles, Thom."

"Take my word for it, Becker. They have wrestling."

"So this Bogan guy, is he tough?"

"Uh, he is extremely tough, and he's mean too... Also carries a sawed-off shotgun and a big old revolver... maybe a three-fifty-seven... and a big knife."

"I think all Australians have a big knife. Seems like I saw that in a documentary."

"Well, avoid him. He's bad news."

At that point, my phone buzzed. It was Tucker.

"I got to run, Thom." I dug in my pocket for my money clip and tossed a fifty on the bar. "Buy a couple of those horny old codgers who survived Miss Faraday a drink on me. And give me a call if you see that nasty gold digger." I decided to toss another fifty on top of that one. Thom needed to know my request was important.

He quickly snatched up the cash into his big sweaty mitt. "You got it, Becker."

Thom resumed checking on customers.

I left the joint, and fast walked to my car. I caught a phone call from Tucker on the way across the parking lot.

"What do you have, Joe?" I asked.

"We need to meet in the morning. Is your office okay or do we come to your house?"

"Come to the house. I have some updates too. Be there at nine."

"Copy that."

Things just got muddy as hell. I needed to sleep on it before I discussed it with my new colleagues, Daffy and Sylvester... But first I'd soak in the hot tub for an hour with a cocktail and a cigarette. I have some thinking to do.

CHAPTER 6

Becker Residence - Lauderdale By The Sea

Nine AM rolled around at the same time it always does. I was up, dressed, and just enjoying my coffee. Detectives Dip and Shit were late as usual. I made a call to the bakery around the corner and asked them to send a kid over with a couple dozen of their best donuts.

At almost a quarter past the hour, I heard my new colleagues stumble in, attempting and failing to appear sober and ready for work. If you could take a freeze frame photograph of them, they might pass for not having hangovers, but since I could see them in motion, staggering in like two drunk sailors in Singapore, it was obvious they were hung over. What the hell is wrong with these new detectives nowadays? I would still be outside the nightclub, puking in the bushes, and trying to find my car at nine in the morning when I was single. This pair was definitely a couple of pussies.

"Morning, Becker," Dedd mumbled.

"Good morning, gentlemen. Coffee is in the kitchen. Donuts too."

I gave them a few minutes to get coffee and help themselves to some donuts. Donuts are an important staple of the FDA recommended investigator diet.

We grumbled some words at each other until we all got settled around the table. Dedd opened his mouth wide and emitted an extended yawn that continued while he was speaking. "So Becker, did you talk to Vance?"

"Yes, I did. She was a charming lady. Impressive."

"Did she say anything about me?" Tucker interjected.

"No… she didn't mention you. But we were talking business so…"

"Well, if it was just business, I guess it's not weird that she didn't mention me."

I was pretty sure Tucker was pouting. Was he still drunk? I hate a spurned drunk. They get so emotional.

Johnny kneecapped him while he was weak. "She probably has a boyfriend now, Tucker. Why would she talk about you?"

"She isn't seeing anyone, Johnny. We're just on a break. That means we don't see anybody."

"A break means you *are* seeing other people, idiot," Johnny replied without mercy.

I couldn't take it anymore. I had to ask. I knew I shouldn't, but I did. "So I take it you and Vance were once an item?"

Tucker almost started blubbering. "After the big blowup with the crooked politicians, we were talking about getting back together. Then out of the blue, she called it off and wanted to take a break."

Johnny threw his hands up. "She caught you making out with a woman in the DMV parking lot. It was broad daylight… what the hell were you thinking? You don't have the skills to pull a Johnny Dedd move."

"Screw you, Johnny. That was not my fault. I met that woman once before and when she saw me, she just came up and kissed me. It would be rude not to kiss her back."

Dedd pushed the issue. "She said you had your hand on the woman's ass."

"That's just a coincidence. I had an elbow cramp," Tucker said a bit loudly for a normal conversation.

"There's no such thing as an elbow cramp, idiot," Dedd yelled in his face.

Tucker got out of his chair and yelled back, "An elbow cramp *is* a real thing, asshole… A REAL THING!"

Oh shit, they're going to go at it again.

I was ready for them this time. I yanked a leather sap out of my pocket and slammed it on the tabletop with a deafening smack. The crack of leather and lead on wood was so ear-splitting it sounded like a gunshot. It startled both of them out of their bickering.

"What the hell…" Dedd sputtered, holding his ears.

"Knock it off, morons," I ordered. "We have work to do. Leave your California shit in California."

"Sorry Becker."

"My bad, Becker."

I felt like I was back in the old days supervising a salty veteran patrol squad again. Sometimes these two can be exhausting.

I gave them a healthy dose of stink eye and ordered them to sit their sorry asses back down. "We got a lot of shit to go over. Let's stay focused, gentlemen. Is that too much to ask?"

Tucker answered, "No, Becker. We were unprofessional. Sorry. There is a lot of work to do today."

Dedd just sort of nodded. I think his bell was still rung from my unexpected intervention. Of course, Johnny always seems to have a sort of confused and perplexed look on his face.

I began. "I talked to Joan this morning, and I met with a local contact last night. There is some nefarious shit going on, gentlemen, and it ain't pretty."

I ran down what Joan told me about their client and this Igor character, then I detailed what Thom told me about Schuster and Faraday. We all discussed our findings at the Port of Miami and what we knew about Boris.

The longer we talked, the more it was looking like Boris and Faraday used Schuster to be the patsy for a lost treasure scam they put over on a group of the wealthiest people in Los Angeles. Their conduit to the Los Angeles scam was a rube named Dagmaier DuBois, their client. Schuster became a loose end. For some reason, they tortured him, probably seeking information. The only thing that made sense was they thought he told someone else about the scam, someone who knew their names. Someone who had to be silenced.

It was likely that whoever that someone was, went to ground. He or she would be difficult to find now.

Then there was the human trafficking angle… and the boat with bunks for fifty… was that for sex-trafficking-slaves or something else? Then what about the goon, Bogan? What was his angle? Did he get whacked too? Where was he now?

We discussed the pros and cons of the case for over three hours. I ordered in some lunch. Then we continued talking until dinner. I threw together a big bowl of spaghetti and meatballs and we feasted as we continued working.

I noticed over dinner that both of them ate fast. The sign of a veteran cop. You never know when you are going to get called out in the middle of a meal, so you eat as much as you can as fast as you can. It isn't great for the metabolism but it's a habit we all have.

An hour or so after dinner, I could see that the guys appeared exhausted. I made a suggestion. "Why don't you two knock off for the night? I have to check on something and then I'm turning in early. Let's meet at my office in the morning and start with clear heads."

"Sounds good, Becker. I'm beat," Tucker replied.

Johnny ended his day like he started it. With an enormous yawn… he tossed in a thumbs up and headed for the door.

Another day in paradise. I hoped twiddle-dee and twiddle dumb could find their way back to their hotel.

After they left, I fired up the Jag and drove up the coast to the local cop bar in Boca Raton. It was low key, but I knew I could find Officer Thorson there. Maybe he found out more since we talked.

The Blue Cat Grill

The Blue Cat Grill didn't really grill much. The hole-in-the-wall joint is a cop bar that serves random bar-food-like substances to anyone drunk enough to eat it. But its focus is on booze.

Cops from all over Broward County have been hanging out there for years. The Blue Cat has all the necessary accouterments of a cop bar, a photo of a beloved patrol sergeant who had passed, a poster of Broderick Crawford standing outside of a patrol car, and a big picture of John Wayne as a Seattle PD cop centered above the bar. There were the standard issue cop groupies and police fans intermixed with real cops who were enjoying an evening off duty, and cops who just got off work.

The crowd seemed to be a pleasant mix of young officers and old retirees. Quite a few attendees dressed in a white t-shirt, dark blue trousers, and black commando boots, or as we used to call it, a policeman's tuxedo. Those were the ones I previously mentioned who just got off shift.

I wandered around the place for a few minutes, squeezing between bodies, before spotting Eric with a couple of attractive women at a corner table. I walked over while absorbing a few arm punches and 'how-ya-beens 'from old-timers who recognized me.

Ferdy Fenderhart, the bartender emeritus of the joint, spotted me too. He'd been there forever and had to be at least a hundred years old... but he was still wiry, so why risk replacing him with someone with less experience? I flashed Ferdy a thumbs up and then pointed to Eric's table. I added the hand signal for a fresh round, too. He knew I would want a Don Camilo tequila neat with a lime twist. It's what I always have when I'm here. I don't remember how that habit got started, but I'd been doing it for thirty-five years in this place.

Eric waved and invited me to sit down at his table. He had a hottie on each side of him. One seemed to be an off-duty police officer and the other simply a loyal fan of law enforcement.

Eric introduced me, "Ladies, meet Becker, the original kick-ass-and-screw-the-names super-cop of Broward County."

The female officer preempted my pending attempt at modesty. "I've heard of you, Becker. You just killed a guy a year or two ago, didn't you? Righteous shooting...very bad ass... old guys are hot!" She leaned over and blatantly checked out my ass... which is a very fine ass, if I do say so myself.

I responded to her comment on the shooting. "I was lucky that day."

"You might get lucky again, big man," she said as she ran her fingers through the hair on the back of my neck.

She seems nice!

"You have an hour to stop that before I put you over my knee," I threatened with a dirty grin.

"Give me the accelerated plan, Becker... this is getting interesting."

I had business to attend to, but I hate disappointing fans. I gave her a card. "Next time you are in my neighborhood, I'll buy you lunch and tell you all about the old days, sweet stuff. But now I got to talk to Eric if I can borrow him for a few minutes."

She faked a good pout, grabbed her groupie pal, and headed for the ladies 'room. Chasing her off wasn't a male or female thing, it was senior professional versus up-and-coming rookie thing. She recognized it and respectfully gave us some space.

I got directly into business. "Eric, did you get anything yet on Schuster?"

"Yeah, sorry, Becker, I got busy and forgot to call. I figured I'd be working in your neighborhood tomorrow and would look you up. But I *do* have something."

"No worries, brother. What did you pick up?" I fondled my cocktail as we talked, but didn't take a sip yet.

Eric answered, "There *is* a daughter. She goes by Evelyn Sutter, a well-to-do and respected pediatrician living in Pasadena. According to the medical examiner, she's being difficult. She disowned her father decades back, hates his guts... you know how that story goes... She wants nothing to do with him and refuses to pick up the body. I think what's left of Schuster might end up in Potter's field, if you know what I mean."

"I'm old... I get the reference... so you think the girl is a dead end?"

"She doesn't seem to be close to this, Becker. My guess is the only benefit to you of talking with her is to get access to any safe deposit boxes or bank stuff he might have. But you're the detective. Maybe there is something there. I'll text you the name and information."

Eric picked up his phone and sent a text my way with an attachment. I looked at it on my phone. All good.

"And there was something else," he added as he shoved his phone back in his pocket.

"What's that?"

"The medical examiner says whoever tortured him didn't kill him."

"What?"

"Yeah, they definitely tortured the hell of out him, but then he died of a massive coronary. He had a heart attack while he was getting tortured."

"So he might not have given them what they wanted," I mused.

'Definitely. They said he went quick... which was probably good for him, considering what the rest of his brief life was going to be like. They messed him up pretty bad, Becker. Like animals. But the medical examiner says he thinks they were just getting started."

"Damn... Schuster was a rat bastard lying asshole, but he didn't deserve that. It's surprising he didn't give up the information right away. I never saw him as having much in the way of guts. But I guess he knew what was coming if he *did* talk, so..."

"Seems that way," Eric said.

The two girls were heading back to the table, so I thanked

Thorson for the lead. "Another case of beer for you when you swing by next time, Eric. Much appreciated."

"You got it, Becker. Anytime… glad to help."

I stood up with my tequila in hand, ready to finish it. The hot female officer slapped me on the ass. I didn't mind it much.

"Hey Becker, not so fast… how about drinks some evening instead of lunch?" She gave me her best semi-drunk come hither look.

I downed my tequila in one gulp, slammed the glass on the table, and locked eyes with her. "Anytime, hot stuff. But bring your friend too. I don't think just one of you can handle me." I returned the slap, planting a good one on her shapely young bottom, if you consider mid-thirties young. I do… it's all relative.

I saw Thorson spit a mouthful of beer out, laughing. I winked at him and left with the girls standing open-mouthed, not knowing what to say. Who knows, maybe those two women will show up one of these times. I might be considered old by some, but I'm very experienced… I'd be happy to show them a good time. They definitely wouldn't forget it.

Ferdy the bartender witnessed the whole thing. He was pointing at me and nodding from across the room while mouthing the words, *the older the bull, the stiffer the horn*. I returned the finger-point like I was Jordan acknowledging an assist after a slam-dunk.

I left the bar in a great mood and walked out into the parking lot and a warm tropical evening. I put the top down on the Jag, lit a cigarette, and enjoyed the cruise home in the cool evening air, smiling at the story Thorson would tell about me and the girls in the squad room tomorrow.

I stirred enough shit for one day and I did it well.

I love Florida.

The Offices Of Becker Investigations

I was up at six and on my second cup of coffee. I sent the information on the Sutton woman to Joan Vance in Los Angeles. It was still way before office hours there, but there was no urgency. They could run her down later and see if she could provide any leads for us on Schuster's death.

Giggle and Piggle showed up around nine and they looked in pretty decent shape for a change. I was a little sad I couldn't bust their chops for being pathetic.

"Good morning, Becker," Tucker said, speaking clearly rather than mumbling. It was unnerving to hear him so coherent in the morning.

"Welcome aboard, gentlemen. Coffee's on. Time to get to work."

Dedd was in a remarkably good mood. "Top of the morning, Becker. It's time to kick ass for America."

"Every time is time to kick ass for America, Dedd," I responded.

"Damned right," he exclaimed as he poured a big mug of hot coffee.

I wasn't sure what brought on Dedd's patriotic surge of enthusiasm for justice and America. But I liked it.

We got straight to business. I told them what I had learned since our last meeting. I told them about Schuster's demise.

Dedd's mood quickly changed to solemn. "You know, Becker, you really have to gauge the guy's health when you apply pain. That's why you start out slow and see what they can take... unless circumstances dictate otherwise."

"And you know this because?" I asked, not confident that I wanted to hear the answer.

Dedd looked at me while he took a long drag on his cigarette. "Yeah. Because."

Johnny stared through me with that 'dead eyes' look he gets sometimes as he blew a smoke ring that might have been aimed in my direction. I felt like he was done explaining. Something about Johnny was unnerving when he got that way.

Nevertheless, our resident psychopath had a point, a creepy point, but a legitimate observation. I moved on to our next lead.

"We have a goon to find," I said, as I tried to put Johnny's dark comments behind me. "He might be dead. He might be alive. It's a toss up. Here's what we got on him." I handed them each a printed work sheet on Bogan, the Australian goon who worked for Schuster. "He's our morning target. Whoever finds him calls the others and we converge before making contact. All good?"

Dedd was on it. "Absolutely. We'll dig him up."

I continued, "Johnny, take my old Ford. Tucker, take your rental car. We all hit the street in twenty minutes."

My two associates were agreeable to the plan. They finished their coffee and left to work the leads I outlined for them in the worksheets.

That felt good. It was almost like back in the old days at the detective division squad briefing. Some days it was all grab ass and bullshit, but most days it was taking notes and getting down to business. I missed all of it.

While they looked for Bogan, I decided to follow up on Goldie the gold digger, also known as Jeanine Faraday. I needed a new strategy with her. Following her didn't work, the Johnny Dedd charm didn't work, so I decided to try direct confrontation. We had little to lose with just talking to her, and another night of following heat runs across south Florida didn't seem to be a wise use of our time.

I knew I couldn't deal with her on an empty stomach, so I wheeled into Ernie's again for a couple of pancakes and some bacon. I swore I saw Ernie disappear out the back door as I went in the front. The grill cook was pulling double duty as waiter and cook. He didn't look happy about it either.

I placed my order. He nodded and grunted, and scribbled it on a piece of paper. I prefer that kind of service to one of those yuppie waiters who pretends as if they like you but then doesn't write down my order. This way has an air of honesty and integrity about it. He wrote down what I told him. He probably hates my guts, and doesn't care if I know it. I call that ambiance.

Before long, the cook delivered a plate of delicious looking high fat and cholesterol food. A perfect breakfast according to the FDA food tables I learned as a kid.

I planned to think about the case while I ate, but my thoughts kept drifting back to Dedd and Tucker... I envied their youth. The late thirties were when I was in great shape and had the experience to quit doing so much stupid stuff. I had to wonder if I stayed too long at the party. Maybe it was time to hang up my guns and do something else... but what? Is there a job out there for a guy who is good at tracking down dirtbags and beating information out of them? Is there a career for someone who can draw a heavy caliber automatic and empty the magazine into a target the size of a human heart in the blink of an eye?

Maybe, but not for someone in their very late sixties... Screw it. I can still do my job. I just need a little more time to climb stairs and I need everyone to clean up their diction so I can hear them better. I have another ten good years of work left in me.

Maybe I should ponder the case rather than the complexities and challenges of a being a geriatric detective... I could do that after breakfast.

I noticed the pancakes were thicker and tastier than normal. "What the hell did you do to the pancakes?" I yelled at the cook working the grill. "They are better than normal."

He yelled back, "I pour a beer in the batter when I make it now."

"You always pour a beer in the batter mix."

"I mean two beers."

A long ash fell off his cigarette and landed on the pile of sizzling bacon. No harm, no foul. He kept cooking and ignored it.

"Does Ernie know you do that shit?" I asked.

"What shit?"

"Adding another beer to the batter."

"Fuck Ernie."

Good talk.

He went back to cooking breakfasts. The discussion was apparently concluded. Never argue with the man at the grill. I believe that's in the Bible.

With about four big bites of pancake and one slice of thick black bacon left, I began developing my strategy for approaching Jeanine Faraday, AKA Goldie, AKA the horny gold digger, AKA the crazy gold digger. She would be cagey, but she might lead us to our bad guy.

My cell phone rang. I glanced at the number... it was Tucker.

"Becker," I answered.

"We got Bogan spotted, Becker. He's at the Surfside Lounge off of Sunrise Boulevard."

"I know the place. That joint's a dump... On my way... don't do anything until I get there."

I threw a fifty on the table and dashed out to my car. I heard the cook ask if I wanted my change, but he didn't say it very loudly.

The service, the no talking - just feeding, was worth a forty-buck tip in my book. No regrets.

I sped down Ocean and shot up Sunrise like a bullet. I was a little concerned that Tucker, with his bad lung, and Dedd, with his lack of restraint issues, would screw this up. We needed Bogan alive and talking.

As I drove west, I tried to mentally picture the place. I hadn't been in it since I was a cop, but it was one of those old shithole bars that seems to be eternal. As I recalled, it was the end unit of a strip mall near a long lake on the other side of Federal Highway. Another thirty seconds and...

Oh shit!

The parking lot was long and narrow, but it seemed to be wide enough for a forty-man brawl. And apparently, the Surfside Lounge had become a gay bar since I last checked it out.

I had no idea that Bogan was gay. I thought he was Australian.

Tucker and Dedd were fighting twenty-to-one odds as Bogan and his friends tried to mob and kill them. I saw Bogan break and run northbound towards the lake. For a big man, he could haul ass. He was wearing loose-fitting black jeans, a long sleeve dark blue shirt with the tail out, and some kind of black running shoes. He was more prepared for a foot pursuit than I was wearing my Brooks Brothers suit and black leather dress loafers.

I had to ask myself a question. Do I save Tucker and Dedd or go after Bogan? Some of the attackers looked like typical Fort Lauderdale 'bro's, but quite a few of them were uniquely flamboyant, including a few cross-dressers, and a handful of very butch lesbians. No matter what they looked like, they were pissed off and could fight like hell. Detectives Shit and Stain were in trouble.

I have a boat. I've mentioned that before. What I didn't mention was that I have an extra boat horn in my car under the seat. The powerful compressed air horn has come in handy a few times in violent crowd situations. The volume of sound it generates is intense, loud, and disruptive to the thought process.

I drove into the middle of the fray, trying to minimize any potential damage to my car, put the transmission in park, stood on the car seat, and blasted the horn for a solid ten seconds. It seemed to stop the fighting as everyone was busy covering their ears and cursing me. I pulled the Sig out of my custom shoulder holster and waved it around like I might or might not be threatening someone. Pro-tip, always leave room for doubt when committing aggravated assault.

"Get in the car, assholes!" I shouted at Johnny and Tucker. They quickly complied for a change and double stacked their sorry asses in the passenger seat as I backed up and out of the battlefield, still waving the gun.

We had been surrounded, but the attackers were losing their blood lust and only lurched along after us, not quite running but not really quitting either. I gave the horn another four-second blast.

They started backing away from us now rather than following.

That's always a good sign.

I gave the two idiots an update and an ass chewing as we escaped certain death... or at least a severe ass kicking. "Bogan sprinted North. What happened to *wait until I get here?*" I yelled as I speed-backed through the parking lot.

I put the Jag into a bootlegger spin, corrected direction, and sped down the alley towards the place I last saw Bogan running.

Tucker was shaken up, "I can't believe that happened, Becker... They just came out of nowhere like some zombie movie."

"What did you do?"

"We didn't do shit," Dedd protested.

"What did you do, assholes?" I repeated myself. I don't enjoy repeating myself and I think the two morons in the front passenger seat quickly figured that out.

Tucker started talking. "We were just going to scout the joint when one of the better looking women hit on Johnny, so Johnny asked him... at least it turned out to be a him, about Bogan, then we figured out it was a dude, there was some words exchanged, uh... unfortunate words.... then things got out of control. Apparently, that guy had issues with rejection."

"Not judging, Becker, I just don't play for that team," a clearly rattled Johnny Dedd explained. "I don't care who is gay as long as I don't have to be gay."

"These things happen. Don't worry about it. We got an asshole to catch."

We came up to a little park that accessed the lake. I gave them each a direction to foot search, although I debated whether to let them operate unsupervised again. I took the center of the park.

In retrospect, I should have kept the gang together. I found Bogan hiding behind a small block service building. He was huffing and puffing... he was also larger, at least up close, than he appeared when he was running.

"Give it up, Bogan. We just want to talk to you."

"I'm no dog... Who the fuck are you wankers?"

"Consultants, not cops... we just have some questions."

"Not today. Get fucked, dickhead."

I've been punched many times in my long life. I can't say I'm a fan of getting punched. I always try to avoid it. But this one came with such speed I had no time to react. Bogan sprang from the ground and threw a left cross that caught me just below the jaw on my neck. It knocked me on my ass. It definitely hurt. But at least I didn't have a broken jaw.

I was stunned. He turned to run. I pulled the forty-five automatic and yelled, "Stop, asshole!"

Unfortunately, he stopped. I didn't really have good cause to shoot him yet, and I damned sure didn't want to fight him. He turned and started walking towards me. A big knife came out of a sheath under his shirt. Now I had a reason to shoot him, but I still needed to question him about the case.

Bogan grinned as he closed on me with the knife. Facing down a gun was not a problem for him for some reason. Australians are like that.

"You're gonna die, ya dodgy bastard."

I cranked a round off between his feet. It had no effect. I think he knew the score. I wasn't eager to shoot him, and he had no compulsion about gutting me. I was on the ground. He was on his feet. I thought about how curiosity had been driving my interest in the Schuster case and how I was a dumbass.

Then a shadow... something dangerous... something violent. Dedd

Johnny dashed across the park silently as a leopard pursuing a rabbit. He leapt upon a picnic table in one stride and launched himself in the air at Bogan's back, displaying incredible athleticism for a big man. He twisted his body mid-flight and clocked Bogan with a downward elbow strike to the back of the head that carried the force of a freight train.

Bogan flew forward, dropping the knife, and landing on his belly, spread-eagled at my feet. Dedd landed square on Bogan's back, with his full weight driving the air out of Bogan's lungs. I heard ribs cracking.

Dedd wasn't done. He rolled Bogan over, straddled his back and started flurry punching, delivering vicious blows to the head and neck of the big Aussie brute, inflicting flesh-ripping damage.

There was something in Johnny's face. It wasn't the guy I had known for the past couple of days anymore. This was an animal. A killing machine. Something awful.

I could see blood pouring out of Bogan's nose and mouth. In one place, his scalp was ripped open almost to the bone. He rolled Bogan over again on his belly, grabbed a handful of hair, and yanked his head back, exposing his throat.

Johnny screamed, "gimme that knife, I'm gonna cut this prick's fucking head off."

I can't say with absolute certainty, but I am pretty sure Dedd was serious.

Tucker scrambled up breathlessly. "Johnny, calm down… Johnny… we need this one alive. It's cool, he's done…"

Joe's calming words sedated Johnny's violence. I felt like he's done this before… more than once.

A glimmer of humanity appeared on Dedd's face.

His breathing slowed.

The bulging eyes receded.

The raging psychopathic killer that lived just beneath the surface within him was subsiding.

Johnny Dedd, the good guy, was still in there.

A moment later, it was over.

Bogan moaned, "I wouldn't mind talking, mate. Just call off your maniac. He's mad as a cut snake."

I noticed some teeth on the ground in the pool of blood. Bogan was big enough to spare quite a bit of blood before he would croak. No worries, everything was billabong now, very shrimp on the barbie, like they say in Australia. Okay, I don't know jack shit about Australia.

Tucker had a zip tie in his pocket. Smart kid. Must have been a boy scout. He secured Bogan's hands behind his back and sat him upright on the grass."

Dedd pulled a handkerchief from his pocket, wiped his forehead, then rubbed the blood off his hands. Johnny had no remorse or regrets about almost killing Bogan, which he most certainly would have if Tucker hadn't intervened.

"You okay, Becker?" Johnny asked as calmly as if he was inquiring about the time of day.

"Yeah, thanks, Johnny. You saved my ass on that one."

"So, if this asshole doesn't squeal, can I kill him?" Johnny asked. "He's not my favorite Australian."

"Sure, Dedd. But I think he'll cooperate now." I didn't feel like disappointing Johnny at the moment. I had a new respect for his reputed hair-trigger extreme violence mode. I just saw it. I still can't quite believe the level of sheer unrestrained savagery I just witnessed, but I was also grateful that he saved my life.

For some reason, I was compelled to ask Johnny a question. "Who *is* your favorite Australian?"

"All of them, except this one. I like Australians."

Fair enough.

I stood up and brushed the dirt off my suit, straightening my clothes. I picked up the knife, squatted down in front of Bogan, and put the point of the blade in his nuts. "I have some questions, fucker. But if you get rowdy, if you withhold information, if you lie, I'll cut off your balls and let this guy over here beat you to death. Do we have an understanding?"

"Sure mate, fair dinkum."

I'm guessing that meant, okay. "Good. Let's start with Schuster. You work for him."

"Not anymore, mate, he's fuckin' dead."

"You did work for him."

"Only when he was alive."

"Yeah, I got that part. Who whacked him?"

"Whack?"

"Who killed him?"

"I suppose it was either that gold digging sheila or her boyfriend had him killed. I don't think they did it personally though."

"What sheila?"

"Faraday, Jeanie or Jenny... Jeanine... he called her something like that."

"Who is her boyfriend?"

"A scary bastard... Boris Komatski. It was probably his mongrels who did the deed."

"Why do you say that?"

"Schuster got greedy. When he saw the tally on the scam they all pulled, he ran to Komatski, wanting a bigger piece of the pie. Shit, the bastard was close to forty million. They thought they'd only get a couple of million out of it at best. Who knew those rich Los Angeles blokes were so stupid?"

"What did Komatski tell him?"

"Something about a deal's a deal and some terrorists would rip Schuster a new arsehole if he didn't back off. But Schuster had the money stashed... him being the middleman on the deal, so if they killed him, they wouldn't get it. He got cocky."

"So, what happened?" I pressed.

"Who knows? He's a Dingo who's backed out on a deal. I could see what was going to happen next. I told that bludger to go fuck himself and I quit. I'm heading back to Australia as soon as I can get some quids. Can I bot some cash as a loan?"

I slapped him across the face for asking, although I wasn't entirely sure *what* he asked. I don't speak Australian. But sometimes a decent smack will reestablish the pecking order in these interrogations. That's Detective 101.

He took the slap and didn't complain. I respect that.

Bogan wiggled his jaw and then began talking again. "Fine mate, I cooperated... Just let me go back to the pub. I was about to convince a sheila in there to loan me some money to get home before you wankers showed up." He grinned with the teeth he had left. "The women in there are crazy about me."

Tucker broke the sad news, "Sorry, Bogan, that sheila was a bloke."

I think he was what we here in the states call *'astonished as fuck.'* Bogan was clearly not happy to receive this tidbit of news.

"The hell you say?" Bogan blinked in confusion a couple of times before his jaw dropped.

Dedd grimly stated, "No, he said it."

Although I suspect that Dedd is a likable and highly functioning psychopath, I noticed that even *he* felt some level of overt sympathy for our prisoner in this situation. I guess Johnny *did* almost fall into the same trap, so it makes sense.

Bogan appeared confused. "Bugger all... are you sure, mate? I've been hiding out in that shit hole a few days now. The place was gobby heaven and I never even had to buy a drink. I never seen anything like it before."

Tucker added, "If you got past second base, you would have had a had a handful of snag, mate."

I didn't know what a snag was, but I guessed what he meant. Who knew Joe Tucker spoke some Australian?"

"Fuck me dead... But she was a stunner, mate. How could that sheila be a bloke?"

Now I was confused too. "So, you're not gay?" I asked.

Bogan was utterly confused. "Gay? Ya mean a poofter, mate? No... what the fuck all makes you think that?"

I wasn't sure what to say. I just shrugged. It appears Bogan's situation was just another tragic case of cultural confusion and low standards.

Tucker interrupted, putting us back on course. "Where is the forty million now?"

Bogan was happy to talk about anything else at this point. "I overheard Schuster say it was in a safe place."

"Where though?" Tucker asked.

"How the hell should I know? I was just an employee, like a bodyguard, mate. I never saw any money. Do you guys work for the Russian?"

I was now even more confused. "What Russian?"

"The California Russian. He's pissed off. He's supposed to be in South Florida now, looking for his part of the money. I think he was in for a ten million dollar loss. He's an evil bastard, they say."

Tucker, Dedd, and I exchanged an *'oh shit'* look. If the guy Bogan was talking about was the lone surviving Russian involved in the Eagle Rock slaughter, if that was even a true story, then he was nobody to fuck with. This did not sound promising. I thought perhaps since the Russian hadn't murdered Dagmaier yet, he might still be open to a recovery solution to the missing money rather than just straight-up revenge. Or possibly the dumb fuck thought the gold treasure really existed and was trying to get it. Who knows? The west coast Russian mob was known for being cagey and extremely violent, but never known to be particularly smart, with a few exceptions.

I wasn't happy with how this case was going and now I had to decide what to do with this Australian hoodlum. I could be described as a disgruntled detective, or maybe I'm just running out of shits to give and want to put this mess behind me. But curiosity had me stapled to the page, and I knew I wasn't going anywhere until this thing was over.

"Is it possible that the Russian killed Schuster?" I asked the big Aussie wrestler turned goon.

"I think Schuster was already dead when he got here. Somebody beat him to it."

It was time to toss him an open-ended question. "So, what the hell is going on then, Bogan?"

He was happy to answer, but he lowered his voice to a whisper before speaking again. "Listen, mate, Komatski works for terrorists. He's using the treasure scam to fund an operation for them to get an even bigger payoff. Komatski used his girlfriend to recruit Schuster into being the face of the scam, since Schuster already had a couple of California connections. It went better than expected, but now the money is in the wind and everyone is pissed off, Schuster got himself killed, and I'm homesick for Oz, mate."

"Who are these terrorists?" Dedd asked. He seemed more serious than usual when the term 'terrorist' came into play. I don't think Johnny Dedd cares for terrorists.

Bogan answered, "I don't know, just terrorists. Some kind of Al Qaida bastards as far as I can tell ya, and I know fuck all about what the hell is going on."

Australians cuss a lot, I recalled hearing. Bogan proved this to be true. Luckily, so do I. I felt like there was no benefit to having this turd in America and it might be in everyone's interest to release him back into the wild of his native land. The smart move would be to let the Aussies deal with him rather than have Johnny whack him here in the middle of an investigation and create potential legal problems for us at some point.

"Do you have a passport?" I asked.

"Yeah, in my pocket, mate." Bogan gestured with his chin towards his left front pants pocket. He was stupid, but not stupid enough to make a furtive move and get himself shot.

"Then get on the next plane to Oz and consider yourself deported for life from America. Cut him loose, Joe."

Tucker flicked a knife out of his pocket and cut the zip ties. A calm and subdued Bogan got to his feet and rubbed his wrists, getting some circulation going again.

Ripping ten Benjamins out of my money clip, I gave our Australian asshole a thousand bucks and called him a ride-share to Fort Lauderdale International. I also gave him a firm warning.

"Look Bogan, If I find out you didn't leave town on the next available flight, I'm having this son of a bitch murder you," I pointed to a smiling Johnny Dedd.

Bogan got the message loud and clear. "Fair dinkum, mate. I'm gone. This town is going to turn into a bloodbath, anyway."

I peeled out another three hundred bucks and stuffed it in his shirt pocket. "Food and incidentals."

"You won't see me again, mate. And, if you don't mind, let's not be talking about what happened back at the bar, okay?"

"Deal. So long, Bogan. Don't come back."

He nodded, turned, and taunted towards the road to wait for his ride, scratching his head and probably wondering what the hell had just happened to him.

Three minutes later, our goon was in the back of a hybrid ride-share car on his way to the airport.

I hoped that was the last we'd see of Bogan, and I think it is fair to say he hoped that was the last he would ever see of us too.

Tucker, Dedd, and I parked our asses at a picnic table in the park. I was still too tired from all the action to walk back to the car yet, and it seemed like a good idea to give the crowd at the Surfside Lounge a little more time to cool off before driving back in that direction. Johnny fished a flask out of his jacket pocket and passed it around.

I'll be very candid. I'm feeling pretty old right now.

Dedd lit a cigarette and gazed back towards the bar. "I don't think we are their favorite detectives."

Tucker replied, "No shit. That place is definitely off the pub crawl list."

I asked, "Joe, where did you learn that Australian slang?"

"Oh, I used to date an Australian flight attendant. She was nice. A beautiful woman."

"I thought you had something going on with Vance?" I asked, somewhat curious, and also somewhat being a dick, just to see the reaction.

Dedd interjected, "That Vance thing is on again, off again, Becker... he keeps screwing it up."

"Well, she's the one, in my book," Tucker sighed wistfully. Perhaps a bit too wistfully for a man... I think Joe's a bit on the sensitive side.

"What happened to the Australian flight attendant?" I

probed.

Tucker began spinning a tale that sounded vaguely familiar. "Oh, you know women, Becker. Even though we were in love, she accused me of making out with some other flight attendant she saw me kissing at the airport. It wasn't my fault *at all* this time. I was minding my own business, when for no reason this Japanese flight attendant I barely knew walked up and kissed me. It would be rude not to kiss her back. That's just good manners, Becker. And I only had my hand on her ass because my arm was tired... you know I am partially disabled, right?"

"Right... isn't this situation the same as that other..."

He cut me off and continued his story. "So, anyway the Australian woman, Ava was her name, who I was in love with, sees us and she jumps to a bunch of ridiculous conclusions. She didn't even listen to my explanation... and while she's yelling at me for that, she started accusing me of a bunch of other stuff I did, and so we broke up. Nobody could see that coming. I have no idea why she thought any of that was my fault. That break up is on her, really...women, who knows what they think... You know what I mean, Becker. You've been there."

I might have involuntarily eye-rolled. "Totally unrelatable, Tucker."

Dedd replied, "I know, right?"

I knew there and then Johnny didn't completely understand what 'unrelatable' meant.

"Yeah, I meant..." I began to correct the record.

Dedd cut me off this time and continued to back up his cousin's sentiments. "Women always jump to conclusions like that. It happens to me all the time too."

I didn't know exactly how to respond to that, so I just went with, "Life can often be quite unfair. It's sad really."

Dedd nodded in agreement, missing the sarcasm.

Tucker changed the subject. He looked concerned. "What do we do now, Becker?"

"For one thing, we avoid that Russian son of a bitch from

California. And for another thing, we need to find that forty million. The only person who *might* know where it is, is Jeanine - the so-called gold digging whore - Faraday. I have a feeling she is up to more than we thought in this thing. I don't think she'd hesitate to throw old Boris under the bus if she could figure out how to pull it off."

Dedd turned pale. "I'm not getting mixed up with that woman again. She's dangerous! How about I take care of the terrorists?" He handed me the flask. I took a sip.

"We won't send you in undercover again as a boy toy, Johnny," I assured him. "We'll try to scam the scammer. But we need to avoid those terrorists, if they exist. That might be a matter for the police department to deal with."

Dedd was unusually insistent. "I don't like terrorists."

"Duly noted, Johnny. But let's stick to the case. When we get this wrapped up, then we'll worry about terrorists." I gave both of them a stern face as I handed the flask to Tucker. "But let's make sure we don't get into any more rough stuff. I don't want to have to file charges on you for abusing a senior citizen."

"You hold your own, Becker," Johnny said smiling, as he took the flask from Tucker.

That was nice to hear. "Thanks, maybe on the outside, Joe. But on the inside, I should be in the back of an ambulance." I shuffled a smoke out of a deck of Lucky Strikes and lit it.

He handed the flask back to me. "Finish it off, Methuselah. This is as close to an ambulance as you're going to get."

I chugged the remaining whiskey out of the stainless steel flask. "Fair dinkum, mate. Whatever the hell that means."

CHAPTER 7

Becker Residence - Lauderdale By The Sea

I t was late, I was sore, and I needed a drink. I poured a hefty serving of Gentleman Jack into a bucket, tossed in a couple of ice cubes, and headed for the hot tub. I turned on my stereo system with an evening mix of Miles Davis and Diana Krall.

So far, this case had turned into what we professionals refer to as a total shit show. I now know who was responsible for Schuster's death, if not the actual murderer. I was looped into a huge California recovery case, which meant recovering money that was probably already spent and gone. I was working with a couple of flaky California private investigators. We had a crazy violent Russian mobster in town up to no good. There was a guy named Boris with a boatload of terrorists involved. And my only reasonable lead was the geriatric nymphomaniac gold digging psychopath, Jeanine Faraday.

So, I've had worse cases.

As I climbed into the hot tub, I noticed the sky was calm and cloudless with just a slight warm breeze coming off the Intracoastal water. I took a sip of my drink and tried to plan out my next moves.

The hot water felt good on my aching body. If I was going to get into any more foot pursuits or fights, I'd have to get in shape, quit drinking, give up smoking, and buy some sensible athletic shoes.

I shook a Lucky Strike out of the pack and considered the folly of unrealistic goals. I have a shit ton of money. I can just hire someone to chase people and fight for me. I wonder what it cost to buy a turd like Tucker or Dedd? Couldn't be very expensive.

I watched the ice cubes melt in my drink, chilling and thinning the bite of the whisky. I pondered what living in a remote cabin in Tennessee might be like. Tennessee is where Jack Daniels comes from. I'm sure it's nice.

But what about this case?

I'd have to talk to Jeanine Faraday. I had to avoid the Russian. I needed to find the forty million bucks.

Speaking of the Russian, I better up my armament game. I had a nice gun collection in the safe. I'd toss the SBR in the trunk of the Jag with some double drum magazines. I'd also have to get my ankle holster and Sig 365 out as well.

I'm not a gun nut, I prefer to think of myself to be a sophisticated weapons enthusiast. I had a buddy of mine in Pella, Iowa build my SBR for me. Ironically, he looks a lot like Tucker, except he's not a puss. My weapon is a short stroke gas piston with a ten-inch FN barrel, made of proprietary "machine gun" metal. It'll run without failing. Melting is not a concern when burning through multiple high-capacity mags. Mine also has a quad-rail fore-end and a muzzle break. I use a Franklin Armory binary trigger, an ambidextrous safety/selector switch, and a non-telescoping brace. Obviously, I had my pal include BUIS (backup iron sight), and a Holosun red dot. My quad-rail allows me to toss on whatever cool stuff I want quickly. I use an inexpensive but functional APEG grip on it, but I have one on most of my few dozen firearms.

The rifle gets the job done at a hundred yards, and with an optic it can reach out and touch someone at three hundred yards... at least that's my personal best at the range, but I wouldn't bet the farm on it in combat conditions.

I'd prefer to have a belt-fed machine gun when things get ugly, but the Sig 220, 365, and SBR would have to get the job done this time. Not saying I can't up the ante quickly if I have to, which might include weapons that are too confidential to discuss.

Hopefully, we can simply take our way through the rest of this goat screw of a case. Guns always complicate things, but it's better to have one and not need it than need a gun and not have one.

In the police force, it was our job to win, not play fair, in violent situations. It's not like we could call 9-1-1... So, I've always felt that the old 'peace through superior firepower' was a very reasonable philosophy, followed closely by that other iconic philosophical phrase, 'peace through superior ass kicking.'

I lit another Lucky, stepped out of my tub, and toweled off while I smoked. It was time to call it a night. Tomorrow might be more productive than today turned out to be. I threw on my lightweight cotton robe and headed up the stairs to bed.

Some people don't care for being alone.

I guess I have learned to prefer it.

Or maybe I just forgot what it was like to have somebody.

The Offices Of Becker Investigations

That famous comedy duo of Rowan and Martin showed up a bit early this time. I better mark that in the calendar.

When I woke up three hours earlier, I had made a decision. We'd work as a team from here on out, no more divide and conquer unless absolutely necessary. I also decided I'd help my California associates up their game with some firepower. Just because they were from out of state, didn't mean they shouldn't be allowed to defend themselves, especially with that Ruskie bastard running around South Florida causing trouble.

I greeted my new colleagues very professionally. "Good morning, assholes."

That got a smile out of Dedd. "Good morning, Becker."

Tucker just threw a half-hearted wave at me.

"If you all are okay with it, I'd like to talk to Jeanine Faraday this morning. I'd also like to help you two get armed in case the Russian starts trouble."

"We're already armed, Becker," Joe Tucker said calmly as he opened his jacket to reveal an old Colt Diamondback.

I was surprised he had a gun and surprised at his choice of weapon. "You don't see guys carrying wheel guns much anymore."

Tucker opened up the other side of his jacket. "I have a Glock 15 too. No sense taking any chances."

"Nice." I respect a man who carries many guns.

Dedd added, "Yeah, Stump sent us a care package. I have a 1911 and a couple of KelTec 32s.

"Oh… that's a very interesting combination. Any long guns?"

"He sent us two Thompsons with some drum magazines," Tucker responded. "He's very old school."

I was impressed upon hearing about the Thompsons. "Those bastards are heavy as hell, but they get the job done. Good choice. Especially in Florida."

"How do you want to approach it?" Dedd asked.

"You two stay close by, use my old car and the rental, I'll drive up to her place in the Jag and try to talk my way inside."

Dedd appeared concerned. "Be careful, Becker. She's scary."

"Not my first rodeo, kid. I'll be fine."

Thirty minutes later, we were staged near Faraday's condo. At this point in the case, there would be no more sneaky shit. We'd just start working it like general detectives and interview our way to the forty million… at least that's what I told myself. In the back of my mind, I couldn't really see how we would get to the money without things getting a little hairy.

The boys were in place and I drove up to her condo and parked on the street out front.

I walked to the door and knocked.

Within a minute, Jeanine Faraday, sometimes known as the dirty gold digging whore, opened the windowless stile and rail door. Even though it was only ten in the morning, she was in full make-up, jewelry, and a black cowl-neck mini cocktail dress that was clearly designed for a much younger woman, yet she made it look like it was made for her. I wondered if the black was for mourning the death of Schuster. It made me wish he had died more often.

I had to catch my breath.

I wasn't prepared.

I should have listened to Johnny Dedd.

I also can't believe I just thought I should listen to Johnny Dedd.

"Can I help you, Mr..." she asked.

"Just Becker, Miss Faraday. May I have a few minutes of your time? I'm a private investigator looking into the death of Charles Brookline Schuster."

"Come in, Mister Becker."

I tried not to stare at her perfectly displayed significant cleavage. I tried not to think about sexy boobs or shapely legs. I'm old, but I'm not dead.

My efforts were failing

Faraday showed me to the front room, and we sat down. Me on a comfortable leather chair and her on the couch behind a cocktail table.

Her condominium was adorned beautifully. It was quite tasteful. I noticed some very refined luxury pieces. I was impressed.

"How can I help you, Mister Becker?"

"Can you tell me about your relationship with Mister Schuster? Was it personal, professional..."

"It was both. We worked together quite often. I'm a consultant."

"What kind of consultant?"

"Just consultant. People hire me. I advise them."

"I see."

I didn't see.

"And you said *both*?"

"Yes, Chucky and I were romantically involved. We even talked about getting married at one point. At least, he was talking about it."

She gave me a smile like that last part meant maybe *'we'* should talk about it. No wonder Dedd was mince-meat in the hands of this woman. She had some hypnotic spell going that put me in a position where it would be difficult to uncross my legs and stand up without revealing her effect on me.

"So, what was the last thing you worked on?"

"We were brokering an investment deal for some high-net-worth individuals from out of state."

"Investment? Like SEC investment? I asked.

"No, simply collectables. Very low key thing. He had some connections, I had some connections, and we were able to put some buyers and sellers together. Our commission would have been significant. But then he was killed, and that was the end of the deal."

"Who were these buyers and sellers?"

"I'm afraid that's confidential, Mister Becker... would you like a drink?"

I knew she was trying to break the rhythm of my interrogation, which is really what this chat was. But a drink sounded reasonable. After all, you can't break a case standing on one leg, can you?

"Sure... I'll have whatever you're having."

"Bloody Mary, dear... I have my housekeeper make some up every morning before she leaves. It's really the only way to start the day, with a healthy breakfast."

"I couldn't agree more."

Dammit, she was charming and funny. Why did this evil woman have to be so attractive and personable? My life sucks.

Tucker and Dedd were listening in to this conversation from my phone link. I was afraid this situation could go south, and

I wasn't crazy about the idea of them hearing it. My personal defenses, self-discipline, and professionalism might not be enough to save me from this woman. Maybe if I think about baseball.

She returned with two nicely trimmed Bloody Marys. In my professional opinion, each drink was a triple, which was acceptable. I'd only have one. But she couldn't weigh more than one-hundred-and-eighteen pounds, so I wasn't sure how she would fare.

"Thank you." I took a sip.

"My pleasure, Becker. You know, I've heard of you. Chucky said you were bad news... a violent man... a little dangerous. Don't you find danger to be a bit of an aphrodisiac? I know that I do." She stirred her Bloody Mary with her fingertip, then slowly sucked the remnants clean from her perfectly manicured digit.

That was intense.

Then she looked at me and licked her moist lips like I was a Mangalitsa pork chop.

Oh, hell.

"Do you enjoy that rough stuff?" she asked with a sly smile.

"I don't think I understand what you mean by that," I lied. Her intent was obvious.

"Oh, I think you understand, Becker. I think you know exactly what I mean." she bit her lips and gave me a cute little feminine eyebrow wiggle. It was meant to have an effect on me. It did. I fought it.

I could see where this was going. She was pulling out all the stops. It was time to play an ace, so I threw the one on the table. "Does the name Boris Komatski mean anything to you?"

"The slap fighting champion?" She asked without reacting in any significant way.

I was surprised my ploy had failed. I was even more surprised she knew about the slap fighting champion. She didn't seem to be the type that would be into that kind of slapping... maybe some other kinds of slapping, perhaps... or for certain...

Is it warm in here?

She wasn't making it easy on me, but I tried to play it cool. "No, Vasily Komatski is the slap fighting champion. He's Polish. This guy is a Ukrainian." I made up the Ukrainian part on the fly. I had no real idea of where Boris was from. I was hoping she might accidentally correct me on his nationality if I was wrong, as people tend to do when you make an error. But I wasn't that lucky.

"Then no, I've never heard of him," she stated flatly.

When a broad lies, and you *know* she is lying, and she *knows* you know she is lying, her first move will either be a sexual distraction or a subject change. She did both.

Her dress was short, but she casually repositioned herself to inch the hem up her thigh even a bit more. It was a sexy move, not made for comfort. It was intended to send an invitation. A normal man can't resist looking at that extra revelation of legs.

I'm normal.

I felt invited.

Then she changed the subject, completing her tactic and disrupting my interrogation flow. "So how did you know, Chucky? He talked like you used to be friends, but then something happened."

She's good. A distraction mixed with a subtle inquiry.

I brushed the question off, not providing any detail. "We were simply business acquaintances, Miss Faraday."

"Please call me Jeanine," she said as she leaned forward for no reason.

My imagination was unnecessary at this point. Everything topside was clearly in view.

How do I get into shit like this?

How do I get out of shit like this?

I focused on the business at hand, trying desperately to keep my mind off the cleavage. It was difficult. "Jeanine, do you know anyone who might frequent the Port of Miami?" It was another 'fishing trip' question.

"No, not really, just people going on cruises. Why?"

"Komatski has a cargo vessel docked there."

I watched her eyes widen as she realized I knew more than she expected me to know. Then she recovered, realizing that she gave an answer she didn't want to. Faraday gave me a vacant stare. Her voice was calm. "Like I said, I never heard of him."

I stared back.

It seemed like the silence lasted an hour. It was just a few seconds.

I was tired of her games. I suppressed an unwanted primal urge to either belt her one with a backhand or ravage her like some animal. I'm not a woman beater. Woman beaters disgust me, but I *have* been accused of being a serial suspect beater. She was trying to press my buttons and I didn't like it. She wanted to arouse me. She wanted to manipulate me. And she was lying. There was a time to get rough during an interrogation... this wasn't the time... yet. I'd keep pressing buttons and see what lit up.

I spoke next. "Did you know a man named Bogan?"

"Never heard of him, either. Can I freshen up your drink?" Her demeanor transformed. The cold-blooded liar effortlessly glided back into the sexy hostess, suggesting erotic play with every move she made and each word she spoke.

She leaned forward again to take my glass. If she was trying to arouse me sexually, it was working... it was really working well.

I tried to think about the old movie where they had to take the sick dog behind the barn. It worked. I felt like I could stand again. I needed to get the hell out of this place.

I put my hand over the drink. "No thanks, I'm fine."

She leaned back and the awkward discomfort began to subside. I felt like I could stand up again.

"That's all my questions for now, Jeanine. Please call me if anything comes to mind about Schuster's passing." I handed her a business card.

"Must you leave? I was enjoying our conversation." She touched the back of my bicep with a little grip and rub. That area sent a message to my other area and started causing me some problems again.

"I'm afraid I must. I have to catch a flight to California to meet with a Russian gentleman," I lied.

My lie worked. Her eyes widened enough this time for me to see the unspeakable fear at hearing me mention a Russian. From what I've heard about Igor Kuznetsov, he has that effect on people. She quickly recovered.

"Is that your client?" she asked, knowing her eyes just gave away a bucket full of guilt.

I was back in control now. I answered her with all the charm and affection of an IRS agent who knows you fudged your expense account. "Confidential, Jeanine. Thanks for the drink. I hope to see you again sometime."

I showed myself out. She looked like she might puke.

Good.

I drove down the street out of view from her home before contacting the Martin and Lewis comedy show. "I'm clear."

Tucker responded to my announcement, "We got it all, Becker. Nicely played."

There was no time for congratulations. This job was about to break wide open. "She'll be moving. This is too big to risk a phone call over. Get ready to follow her. I think she's going to pay Boris a visit."

"Copy that."

"Copy that."

We were ready for a moving surveillance, and our target was scared shitless and guilty as hell. If Boris wasn't at his boat, we'd soon know where he was.

Taking strategic positions, we played the waiting game. But we only played ten minutes before her car screamed down the street, passing Johnny's car. I wasn't worried about her spotting him. She had some serious stress-induced tunnel vision.

Tucker came on the comms again. "The bird dog is still working. We can run a loose surveillance."

I gave a curt, "Copy that."

Good news. Our little bug, compliments of Johnny Dedd, was still functioning. We were between rush hours, so this should be a straightforward job.

Over the many years I've been doing this shit, I've noticed that criminals are very cagey and clever about surveillance until they really need to be. If they get nervous or rattled, all of their counter-spy trade skills go out the window. The gold digger proved this observation to be true again. She hauled ass to Miami like a fat guy racing to the head of a buffet line, unexpectedly high speed and focused like a laser beam.

The surveillance wasn't bad. Everyone in southeast Florida drives like they have a death wish. The handful of reasonable and cautious drivers on the street are generally killed off before lunch.

There were no surprises until we got into downtown Miami. Instead of exiting to the Port of Miami, she turned into Overtown. Tucker took the eye and trailed her to a large warehouse on the Miami River. It was a two-story block building with a small parking lot for maybe six cars on the east side. The building was painted white and had docks and loading equipment along the waterside.

She parked on the street and ran in, not even checking for cross traffic. I must have really fucked up her day.

Half an hour later, she came back out and got in her car. She didn't carry anything with her that she didn't carry in.

Dedd came on the comms. "What do we do, Becker?"

"Let her go. What we are looking for is probably here. I'd hazard to guess that she's going home to pack a bag and head to the airport."

"Makes sense," Tucker commented.

I made a management decision. "Let's set up on it a while and see what we see."

Our little team of Elwood, Jake, and I took positions and watched for an hour. There was no movement.

I asked Tucker to do a walk by and read off license plates in the small lot beside the warehouse.

He conducted a subtle walk by. I wrote down the numbers and made a call to my pal Dourdhoff Jenkins.

"Jenkins," the obviously electronically altered voice said.

"Turn that dumbass thing off, Jenkins. It's Becker."

"I know who it is. What are you doing in Overtown? Do you hate living?"

"How did you know I'm in Overtown?"

"Duh. You are calling me on a cell phone. You have no privacy, Becker. Not with me or other geniuses like me."

'Right... so, I need some plates and whatever you can get on this warehouse." I gave him the address. "Call me back if you can get it. What's that take, a week or something?"

"Sending you the schematics and ownership records on the warehouse now. Check your text messages. Also, here are the registrations on the cars in the parking lot. The black Grand National is a classic. Will you put a note on it for them to call me if they want to sell it? The guy who owns it needs the money. He's behind in his credit card payments and a month late on rent. He'll need money. I can pay in cash or crypto, whatever is easiest. I can just Venmo the money if that works."

"What in the hell are you talking about... stop talking... what?"

"Keep up, Becker. This is the 2020s, not the 70s... Take one step, drag a Luddite."

"Okay, fine, if we don't have to blow the joint up, I'll leave a note."

Dourdhoff wasn't done. "Hey, it looks like the guy on the lease for the warehouse had a business relationship with a guy who has a brother on the 'no fly' list... probably a terrorist or some shit."

"How do you know this stuff? That's impossible to know that fast."

"If you're not a dumbass, it's easy. Let's grab a burger next week. Thom's place?"

"Sounds good. Oh, I was going to tell you, we need to check out a 1945 Jaeger-LeCoultre Dirty Dozen that Jack is getting in next week from an estate sale. I might make an offer on it if it's in nice condition."

"You and your old military watches... I'd actually like to see it. Call me when Jack gets it in the store. I'll meet you there and then we grab a burger."

"Sounds like a plan."

I disconnected. How in the hell do these computer guys access everything on everyone so fast? It scares the hell out of me. I considered tossing my phone in the river and never touching a computer again.

Tucker came on the comms and interrupted my digital paranoia. "There is a boat pulling up to the back. Looks like a thirty-foot express cruiser."

"Anybody leaving?" I asked.

"No... three guys arriving. It was a drop off," Tucker reported.

"Get the hull numbers. We'll see what happens here."

"Copy that."

"We're going to need a boat."

Dedd responded. "I'm on it."

"No... don't steal one. Johnny. Meet me and I'll give you the keys to my boat. You should be able to get back down here before dark. Get out of the Intracoastal and haul as to Miami down the Atlantic. That will be fastest. When you're close, contact me and I'll vector you back in."

"On my way."

"Keep your guns with you."

"Affirmative."

Twenty minutes later, Johnny Dedd was on the freeway

northbound to pick up my boat.

We started early today so there would be at least six or eight hours of light left before nightfall. I didn't expect anything to happen until dark.

I was right.

Johnny motored into the River an hour before dark and tied up by a waterfront restaurant with a bar. I took the eye. Tucker stayed back, ready to move if they went mobile by land. We had the place buttoned down.

We were in hurry up and wait mode.

I had spent most of my day reviewing schematics of the building, reading background material on the people who were the registered owners of the cars in the lot, and doing a lot of thinking.

I wondered if I should call Maggie. I hadn't talked to her for a while. Maybe she wasn't interested anymore.

Then my thoughts drifted to Jeanine Faraday. That woman knew things about eroticism.... scary things. I'd never run across anyone quite like her.

My mind also wandered into matters regarding the case. Why was I still invested in this? I didn't need a share of the money. My curiosity was satisfied as to who killed Schuster. As it turned out, the prime suspect was cholesterol. But then there was that nutty message. I pulled my leather notebook out of my pocket and reviewed it again... *'If I am found dead by suspicious circumstances, call Becker and tell him it was those guys from California. He will find them. Take in Grande, get to Pas.'*... What the hell does any of that mean? Who is Grande? Why do we need to take him in and get him to Pas? The only two Grandes I have ever heard of are the river in Texas and the donut licking skank in Los Angeles. Neither of which was near Fort Lauderdale.

Maybe it was one of those things I'd never find out.

Before I knew it, the sun was down. I hoped Johnny wasn't

getting wasted.

Tucker made a broadcast. "Movement by the dock behind the parking lot. Six guys. They look like assholes. They are boarding the cruiser. Moving back towards downtown."

Then things started happening. And they happened fast.

CHAPTER 8

I knew the thirty-foot cruiser, with fuel tanks topped off, could potentially get them to Bimini or perhaps further, but most likely they head to a spot along the coast. My bet was, they were going to their transport vessel in the Port of Miami.

If they were going to their freighter, then we might get a closer look at them. I gave out new assignments. "Tucker, stay with the car. We'll need ground transportation when they land. Johnny, I'll meet you at the bar and we will follow them on the water."

"Copy that."

I locked up my car. Being an only slightly less cautious fellow than that guy who changes the lightbulb on the top of the Empire State Building, I also grabbed my weapons bag out of the trunk and joined Dedd dockside on my boat. Amazingly, I don't think he'd been drinking.

He was at the helm when I untied the last dock line.

"How was the bar, Johnny?"

"Nice joint. I got a date with a hot bartender tomorrow night. She couldn't resist the Johnny Dedd charm. I'm one good looking Italian, Becker. Women can't resist me."

"I hadn't noticed."

"It's true," he said, completely missing my sarcasm.

"Did you bring your weapons?"

"Stored in that locker," he said, pointing to a secured locker on the gunwale.

"Good. Let's hope we don't need them."

"I think I heard someone mention terrorists, though."

"We aren't in the terrorist killing business, Johnny. We're in the private investigator business."

"We *are* still Americans, Becker."

"That's why I bought my guns too, Johnny."

Dedd fired up the outboards, and we began following the cruiser. I hoped Boris was one of the six bad guys we knew of who were on the boat. At this point we weren't sure what he even looked like, so hoping was about all we had.

"They're coming out to the Intracoastal," Johnny advised.

"Stay back. Let's see where this leads."

Following a boat on the Intracoastal isn't like following a car. You don't have the dense traffic that can move as fast as one hundred miles an hour. And it's not unusual for two boats to be on the same course for hours, if not days, on end as they move up and down the coast. Even holding binoculars was not unusual. Luckily, I also had AIS tracking and night vision gear. We wouldn't lose them.

"They didn't head down towards the Port of Miami, Becker... where the hell are they going?"

"I don't know. I'd a bet a million bucks they were heading to Boris's boat."

A half hour later, after they transversed the Biscayne Bay and headed to open ocean taking a northerly heading, my gut sank.

They weren't going to their boat. They were going to my house. This was a hit squad.

I'm a dumbass... why did I let her think I worked for Igor? These guys aren't hoods or punks, they are international criminals and terrorists. Am I too old for this game? I must be if I'm making a rookie mistake like this... and now my bad decision could put Tucker and Dedd at risk.

I shared my concern with Johnny.

"I fucked up, Dedd. These assholes are going to my house. I shouldn't have let on to Faraday that I was connected to that looney California Russian."

Unexpectedly, he seemed happy at hearing this news. "Good.

We can whack pieces of shit… maybe keep one alive long enough to get some information. What a great break."

"Uh… they are going to my house. I don't whack people at my house. I don't whack people anyplace."

"I suppose in the strictest interpretation of 'whacked,' that is correct, but I'm talking kill. We need to *kill* them all… especially if they are terrorists, Becker."

I reluctantly concurred. "I don't think they will leave us a choice."

Some days you sit on the patio sipping coffee and waving at your neighbors, other days you blow assassins off it with extreme prejudice.

I got on the phone to Tucker and advised him of the new situation and change of plans. "Joe, get to my house, you'll beat them there. Set up an ambush. There is a concealment safe behind the big portrait of Ronald Reagan in my office."

"Which portrait of Ronny? You got about nine of them in there."

"The big one… with him on a horse and cowboy hat."

"The horse has a cowboy hat?"

"No… Ronny does."

Wait… was he screwing with me?

Tucker confirmed. "Got it… what's in there?"

"Something special. You'll know what to do with it."The best position will be on the bedroom deck. Those decorative panels on the railing are quarter-inch steel, so they'll provide you some cover."

"Copy that."

I made one more call. "Eric, are you on duty right now?"

"Yeah… we're on the water."

"Great. There might be something of interest happening behind my house in a couple of hours. If you can hide over by the boatyard, just listen for the explosion. I'll need it to be a fuel line malfunction, if you get my drift."

"Uh... sure, Becker. Nobody really follows up on our investigations. Homicide doesn't even come out unless it's a celebrity."

"Cool. This will make you a hero... Think 'terrorists' in residential canal."

"Nice. I got it, Becker. Good timing too... I have Mulqueeny and Scott with me this shift. Remember them?"

"Those two no-neck brutes are still on the job?" I laughed at that piece of news. It was a fortunate break to have them around in this kind of situation. They were old-school range instructors, that is, until they were suspended after their fourth officer involved shooting incident during lunch breaks. It wasn't like they were looking for trouble. Those two were violent felony magnets. And they knew how to fight. I suspected that the city put them on one of the boats to keep them out of trouble. If memory served, Scott still held the department record for most excessive force beefs. This couldn't be better.

"Tell them Becker says 'welcome to the party, pal.' They'll know what that means. Thanks Thorson... I owe you one."

Cops are honest, but they are also realists. The good ones know how to make things palatable to the brass and the public, like for instance, sometimes terrorists explode for no reason. That is a circumstance that everyone can live with. Thorson, Mulqueeny, and Scott knew this intuitively. I had no doubt they would get my Christmas movie reference and conclude what the stakes were.

And now the odds were six to six... unless Boris had more guys I didn't know about.

I knew the shortcuts and the places where we could open the throttle up. We'd be there ahead of Boris. My police department marine patrol pal, Tommy Thorson, would be staged and waiting. Tucker should be at his position in the house by the time they arrived.

I hated that my neighbors would have to suffer this incident.

I liked my home. I didn't want to see it shot to pieces and full of dead guys. But if that is what it takes to keep these terrorist supporting assholes at bay, so be it.

We got there faster than suspected. Johnny was a good boat handler and my boat, with its maximum 900 horsepower, was up to the job.

"Johnny, we have maybe twenty minutes until they get here. Tie up at the docks by the officers... over there, near that catamaran."

"Copy that."

I flashed a light at the patrol boat. Tommy returned the signal. Johnny Dedd expertly maneuvered us into a spot that was out of sight and allowed us easy foot access back to my dock or the police boat. The canal I live on is just off the main Intracoastal and ends in a T-shaped configuration providing a nice turnaround for the larger boats that might find their way back here. Some of the houses had sixty or seventy footers back here. Behind the T-shape was a row of commercial buildings which had their back doors to the water but entrances from the street side, including the bakery where I order my donuts and numerous marine vendors ranging from canvas repairs, engine maintenance, to insurance. There was a small walkway combining docks, walkways, and sidewalks that could be maneuvered to get to my place on foot.

I called Tucker on my cell phone.

"Are you ready?"

"Hell yes..." he replied enthusiastically. "I haven't seen one of these since I left the service."

"You only get one shot," I reminded him.

"No problem."

"Then take care of business. The patrol boat is in place. Dedd and I will approach on foot... we have about fifteen minutes now."

"Copy that."

I looked at Johnny. "Let's go meet the boys."

He gave me a thumbs up, then traversed the path with me to get to their boat. We had to cross over a cuddy-cabin and a pontoon to board the hidden police boat.

"Permission to come aboard," I whispered.

Thorson responded professionally to my request, "Granted."

We hopped over the gunwales and onto the deck.

A beast who looked like a homely version of Ernest Borgnine stuck out a fat, calloused paw, "Becker, you piece of worthless shit… I thought you were dead."

I grinned, "Scott, you sorry-assed bum… I heard they had you in a rest home."

An unseen fist tried to punch a hole in my shoulder, followed by a voice that sounded like loose gravel under the wheels of a dump truck. "Becker… how in the hell did you get uglier since I seen you last?"

"Mulqueeny, you fat bastard… you *wish* you were as pretty as me." He had one of those faces that wouldn't notice a few punches. But he can be a beautiful sight to behold when a pack of psycho killers are hunting you.

I exchanged embraces and curses with my two old brothers in blue. They were new guys, maybe just under ten years on the job, when I retired… maybe more, maybe less… who remembers that shit for sure? But we still kicked some ass together on the street. Some of the best men I ever knew.

I introduced my partner. "Men, this is Johnny Dedd… he's that cop from Oxnard PD on the west coast who smoked the child predator in the interview room five or ten years ago."

Scott didn't hesitate. "Damn, man… You know how many times I came close to doing the same thing? Welcome back, brother." He clasped Johnny's hand and shook the living shit out of it.

Mulqueeny was no less hesitant. "Good job, Dedd. I remember reading about that shit. They should have given you a fucking medal."

Thorson, being younger, didn't quite get it yet. He was a little more hesitant. I could see it in his eyes. Tommy Thorson was a bit afraid of Dedd. But that's not necessarily an unreasonable point of view. Hell, I'm a little afraid of him myself. A little fear around a violent psychopath is just good judgement. Thorson avoided the mutual admiration society love fest and got to the point. "Welcome aboard, both of you. What's the gig?"

I gave them a rundown on what I knew so far. If they were going to risk getting killed, they had to be read into the case. But time was short, so I talked fast.

"… and so now I have this Boris asshole making a run at me… I don't know if *he's* on the boat coming in, but he has at least a half a dozen guys on board who are either gun thugs or terrorists. They're coming to take down Casa Becker and it's happening in about five minutes."

"Shit!" Thorson said, a bit wide-eyed as everything suddenly became real.

I could see wheels turning in his head. He had always wanted to be a tough guy, a real cop, a bad-ass, but now the entry fee to the club was due and he was wondering if he had the money in his account to cover it. Everybody wants to be a hero cop until it's time to do hero cop shit.

I saw no such hesitation in Mulqueeny and Scott. Instead, I saw joy in their eyes. A day of reckoning with the assholes of the world was upon us. It was like Christmas for them.

That is the difference between new guys and old guys on the police force. The old guys joined up to fight crime and have some fun, but also wanted a good stable job. The newer guys wanted a good stable job first and hoped to have some fun being a cop as a by-product. I think at some point, you see enough misery on the street caused by assholes and punks who have no regard for the decent people who are just trying to live their lives that you finally wake up. You realize you are the worst thing that will ever happen to these dirtbags… not a judge, not prison, just you, there and then… while you have your hands on them. It is the only time they see immediate and direct consequences for their dirtbaggery and fucktardary. And that, my friends, is when the young officers finally achieve '*old school*' level... no more pussy bullshit. After that awakening, if you see a hood, you make him regret his career choices. No one else will.

I hoped that Thorson, who I considered to be a good guy, would become '*old school*' tonight. He had the right team around him. And besides, my life depended on him doing exactly that.

"Here's the plan," I explained. "Dedd and I are going in on foot. We'll be hiding by the stand of palm trees on the corner of my patio. I have a guy with something special on the upper deck. I suspect these guys will drop a hit team off on my dock. If they are unarmed and we can take them down hand-to-hand, Dedd and I will get them and you back us up. If they come in heavy, I'll kill as many as I can before their boat explodes, then you roll up and save the day."

I could see in their eyes that they knew I didn't expect to take the attackers alive.

Scott spoke up, "So, do we open up on them?"

"Just use the 'defense of third party' rules and your own piss-poor judgement."

That crack elicited a grin and a grunt-like laugh. Third party rules simply means an officer is allowed to use reasonable force up to deadly force, to protect their own life or the life of an innocent third party. Tonight I'd be the innocent third party, a home-owner who happened to be armed when home-invaders assaulted his property. The officers would just happen to be in the area and heroically respond. Third party rules of defense apply.

I added, "Seriously, If I can take them, I will. I'd prefer you just handle the clean up on aisle nine."

"Not a problem. We can make it go away."

We seemed to have a consensus.

I spoke again, this time only addressing my partner on the ground operation. "Let's go, Johnny."

The boat crew, Johnny, and I all knuckle-bumped before Dedd

and I hopped back on terra firma.

I checked my SBR out of habit. I made sure the can was in place to suppress as much sound as possible. Johnny had the Thompson loaded with a one-hundred-round drum magazine which looked like a fat pie plate. We were ready. I couldn't see Joe Tucker, so I calculated that he was doing a very good job of ninja work.

I whispered the plan one more time. "Johnny, I'll see what I can do with the suppressor. You will be backup with that Chicago typewriter in case this gets to the point that noise doesn't matter anymore."

I felt a hand tap my shoulder twice as a confirmation.

Minutes later, the sound of a boat came down the channel. It was running dark. I figured the crew wasn't from around here. A boat running dark in a residential area on the intracoastal will generate calls from homeowners along the water. There are too many burglars pulling shit with that technique.

Running dark is a stupid move.

Maybe these assholes *are* terrorists, I thought. Terrorists are known for doing stupid shit.

I brought my weapon up to the ready and relaxed, keeping loose… preparing to light their asses up when the time came. I began my breathing control technique to calm myself.

The vessel killed its engine and drifted with its momentum up to my dock. Four guys jumped off the vessel and onto my patio. Two other guys flattened themselves on the bow of the boat and took prone defensive positions. Another two guys covered the transom. One asshole remained at the helm.

So there were nine of them.

Time for some fun.

The four-man hit team started to stealth their way to my back door. The dim solar lights in the raised planting beds silhouetted them.

We'd have to be fast. The cover guys on the boat could cut us to shreds as soon as the party started.

I lined up my trademark neck shots.

Breathing.

Pressing.

Repeat.

Pop... Pop... Pop... Pop...

Four bodies slumped to the dock.

As the defenders on the boat tried to figure out what just happened, Dedd and I flattened ourselves behind the palm trees.

Before the assholes from Miami could blanket my backyard with suppression fire, I felt a concussive thump in my chest accompanied by the 'whoosh' sound of the hand-held rocket launcher releasing a projectile towards the uninvited boat.

Perfect timing, Tucker!

The rocket hit near the transom by the fuel tanks.

An explosion.

No... a thermonuclear detonation... at least it felt like that as the blast and heat wave swept over us.

I heard a voice from my balcony laughing and yelling, "Did you see that shit?"

Boris was down one cruiser, and the canal behind my house was lit up like daylight as the boat burned.

Thorson rolled up, or at least figuratively rolled up. He motored to the scene and initiated standard firefighting procedures except rather than dousing flames, the crew used their water cannon to spray a dense wall of cover between the houses across the canal and the burning boat, giving us time to operate unobserved.

Dedd and I sprang up and ran to the downed terrorists. I decided they were definitely terrorists at this point. A quick inspection informed us that my weapons skills were not bad for an old man. Each body had a through and through hole in their neck. Bloodier than I had hoped for, but clean ballistics-free kills nevertheless.

One was still twitching. Johnny jammed his heel down on the

guys larynx.

"Shit, you stomped on his throat," I said for no reason other than I was a little shocked at his brazen cruelty.

"Not the first time."

The guy quit twitching.

Johnny grabbed the first one by the ankles as I grabbed his arms and we heaved him aboard the burning boat. We repeated that process three more times.

I undid their dock lines and let the vessel drift to the middle of the canal. By now, people were coming out to see what would be later reported as a floating meth lab explosion.

The downside of maritime cover-ups is you can't use the venerable 'gas line explosion' excuse. But meth labs are just as explodey, so it's fine.

Our guys on the police boat were able to tow the burned hulk into the bay and away from the residential area. The move would make sense to their bosses, as meth labs are notoriously toxic.

The bad guy vessel, or what was left of it, ended up at the police impound dock where mysterious things occurred. *'Just between us'* kinds of things.

For example, in the darkness, most of the bodies and guns fell off the burned-out boat and miraculously landed on a previously seized cigarette boat that had been awaiting auction on the very remote, and for some reason unsupervised, police storage docks. And even more unfortunately, those bodies were taken fifteen miles off-shore and dumped at sea before the cigarette boat was returned to its proper tie-up.

It was a fit and proper cleanup. All I had to do on my end was hose the blood off my patio and spray a little bleach where the blood pools had been.

I was proud of the marine patrol officers. Thorson became an old school cop tonight. He'd keep his mouth shut. I trusted him.

Meanwhile, back at the ranch, Tucker's erection lasted more than four hours after his first time at playing Battleship with a real missile and a real boat. He did not consult a physician, though.

Dedd was a little depressed he only got to kill one guy.

I was relieved that with minimal work, I was merely a witness to a loud noise and not a suspect in four murders in the police reports. The police marine patrol saw to it. Nobody looked over their shoulders. They were more like pirates in blue, rather than cops, to the department brass. The whole event would '*go away*' as it was scripted.

We fought a lot of crime tonight. I felt like Sir Robert Peale might be hiding his eyes up in that big precinct in the sky, not acknowledging, yet reluctantly approving, of our methods. Why? Because all the community policing and unicorns in the world simply won't work against professional gun thugs and terrorists. It takes good guys who are worse than the bad guys to deal with that sort of threat to the peace and tranquility of the public.

Tonight, we took it to them.

They were rehabilitated.

I wondered if Boris died on the boat tonight, or if this was simply the opening salvo of a very protracted war.

I went inside the house and made a drink.

While I was at it, I made one for Tucker and Dedd, too.

"We won," Tucker claimed as he strode down the stairs, beaming like he was walking out of Air Force One, still a bit giddy from his first successful missile strike.

I wasn't as happy. "We won this, but now our case took two steps backwards. They know we're coming and we burned our only lead."

Dedd agreed. "They'll be coming at us heavy next. We're not just an annoyance, now. We're an obstacle... to whatever the hell they are up to."

"No shit, we need to regroup," I grumbled.

When in situations such as this one, it's often best to drink heavily and reflect on the degree of fucktitude you are facing. We did just that.

I was pouring the fourth round when Dedd came up with a good idea. "Why don't we go find them and kill all of them?"

I wasn't sure we had a choice. They would certainly kill all of us at some point. Plus forty million dollars was at stake, and I don't think any of the parties involved knew exactly where the money was.

We professionals have a phrase describing this type of scenario... and that term is *screwed if you do, screwed if you don't.*

"Let's rethink this from the beginning," I suggested.

"Makes sense," Tucker said agreeably.

Obviously, nobody else had a better idea, so I began.

"I have a dead guy here in Fort Lauderdale who left a weird note that mentioned my name. He is a guy I used to work for named Schuster. Schuster had something going with a gold digger going by the name of Jeanine Faraday. His name pops up in your investigation."

Tucker chimed in. "Check... we get a client, Dagmaier DuBois, who got scammed out of forty-million and is sweating the vengeance of the elite L.A. crowd who financed him."

I took over again. "It seems we have a dirtbag in Miami named Boris Komatski, a polish international criminal who is behind the scam that tagged your client. He might have a thing going with Faraday, too. They might have set up Schuster."

Tucker grinned. "She's Johnny's girlfriend too."

Dedd drew back to throw a punch, but I quickly slipped my forty-five out of my holster and placed it on the table as a warning. "Two of us can finish this, Dedd. Calm down."

The message was received. He got calmer than a sleepy cat in a sunny window.

I continued, "We trail Faraday to a business that might be a front Boris is using, she spills her guts to him about us... and the next thing you know we have a crew of hitters on my patio."

Tucker added. "Don't forget the names the journal we found... That Kruger guy... or Igor the Russian."

Dedd joined in. "We can't forget Mister Igor Kuznetsov... he's a very unhappy Russian. And he's either here, or on the way here, to kill everybody involved in the Los Angeles scam. Maybe including me and Tucker, since we are hiding DuBois."

Johnny said, "A very dangerous and unhappy Russian."

Tucker answered, "The worst kind of Russian."

"I thought we decided that Kruger was the name of the lost gold stash?" I asked, a little lost.

Dedd answered, "Stump found out that there is a big ugly bastard called Kruger who is saying he is a descendent of the original Kruger who lost the gold in the first place. He was a critical part of the scam.

"What an asshole," I said aloud.

Johnny nodded, "I know, right?"

Tucker added, "Plus, that Boris guy might be in cahoots with terrorists. I almost forgot about that."

I didn't want to hear any more crap about Igor, Boris, Kruger, or terrorists, so I started the wrap up. "So the bottom line is, we think Schuster might be the only person who knew where the forty-million is. Boris wants it. Igor wants it back, and Jeanine Faraday will boink anybody in order to beat them to it."

Dedd spoke, "She might also boink anybody who isn't looking for the forty-million. She's scary."

I couldn't disagree that the woman was weaponized sex in stiletto heels. "Maybe so, but she might be our wild card."

"How so?" Johnny asked.

"She seems to be familiar with the Boris operation. She was familiar with the Schuster operation. She might be the only living person who knows the whole story of what these asshats are up to."

Dedd didn't like it. "We got no defenses against her, Becker. The woman is some kind of succubus or black widow or that wormhole woman..."

"Who?" I asked.

"The succubus... or, which one?" Johnny asked, looking a bit lost.

I cut him off, "No… what wormhole woman?"

He elaborated. "The one who murdered all those guys here in Florida… she was a prostitute serial killer?"

I shook my head. "Do you mean Aileen Wuornos?"

Johnny looked at me like he was pissed off that I knew the name and he didn't. "How should I know? I'm not from around here."

"I think you mean Aileen Wuornos… she's not around anymore either."

"Good."

Johnny acted like he just explained it to me instead of the other way around. I hate technical conversations with Johnny Dedd. Why do I let myself get drawn into this shit?

I got our review back on track. "So, we know where we are, now what do we do next?" I asked.

Tucker was remarkably insightful. "We could set up on the business or the freighter in Miami. See what moves they make next."

I posited, "Or we could hunt the woman and see where she goes."

Johnny added, "Or we could just go look for the money. It has to be around Fort Lauderdale someplace. Let Igor take care of Boris and his terrorist buddies."

I couldn't disagree with Johnny's logic. He's not stupid, he's simply more cunning than book smart. Plus, he saved my life, so I really can't get mad at him.

"We can split forces and do all of the above." I suggested.

Tucker didn't like it. "If we are facing down commando hit teams full of terrorists, we might want to stick together. These turds might not be done with us yet. We've never discussed what they're going to do, only what we're going to do. We need to think like assholes if we are going to catch assholes and recover that money."

Dedd and I looked at Tucker with increased respect. He was right.

"So, what do we think they will do next?" I asked. Tucker and Dedd were much better at thinking like an asshole than I am... I'm usually pretty good at thinking like a bad guy, but they are true grand masters of assholery.

Tucker expanded on his idea. "I think they aren't going anywhere without the forty million. Neither is that scary woman. I don't think they know about Igor. So, my guess is they will do the same thing we just did, start at the beginning."

"The warehouse?" Dedd asked.

"Yeah. I think they will figure out their hit crew got whacked and they'll send a team to the warehouse, to Schuster's house, and then maybe lean on the gold digger."

"That sounds reasonable," I mused out loud.

Tucker said, "So, let's do this. Why don't we saddle up, run over to the warehouse. and see if they show up? What could go wrong?"

"Everything," Dedd grumbled.

Tucker frowned. "Then what do you suggest?"

"I'm not disagreeing. I'm just saying a lot could go wrong. Less might go wrong if we go to where we know they are, that place on the river, and just ask them where the hell the money is. That will get them off our back because they'll know we don't know. They can focus on killing people besides us. It's a survival thing, really. Then, we figure out which one is Boris and follow his dumb ass."

"That ain't bad, Johnny," I said, fully impressed with his theorizing. "In fact, that makes pretty good sense. We take the game to them." I was finally appreciating the value-add of having Johnny Dedd on a team, besides just his violence and psychopath part.

"But we might have already killed Boris, if he was on the boat," I said.

"I don't think he was."

"Why?"

Johnny explained, "One, most of those guys, at least the ones we could see, were younger assholes. I feel like Boris is older if he is running around with the gold digger and if he built a world-wide criminal organization… that takes time and experience. Two, he has enough torpedoes to take care of loose ends. If he is as big an operator as we think, he'll stay focused on finding the money. He wasn't on the boat. He's back at the riverfront building."

Tucker caught the spirit too, "Let's have two of us go in and tell them their guys killed our third partner… then we can have someone completely off the table they don't know about."

"Wow. Again, not bad," I said.

Tucker gave credit where credit was due. "I saw it on a John Wayne western. Duke told the Paladin dude that one of their guys was dead, but he was really alive… he was a sniper and was hiding in reserve in case the deal went south."

I looked at Johnny. "Weren't you a SWAT sniper?"

"I was," he said proudly.

"Are you still any good?" I asked.

"Is the invisible man waterproof?" he answered confidently.

I wasn't certain of what I just heard. "What? Are you sure you mean…"

He cut me off.

"I'm still as good as ever, Becker. Don't worry about it."

"Fine… Do you have a rifle with you here?"

"No.. but I can probably find one."

I saw the wheels rapidly turning in Johnny's head, calculating how he could procure a sniper rifle, so I suggested a selection from my vault rather than risk his head exploding. "I have a Barrett 50… is that too big?"

"Not big enough, but I'll make it work," he answered with the grin of the devil farting on a stack of lost souls. "What optic does it have?"

I didn't have a Beelzebub grin like Johnny, but I did feel an 'Old Testament vengeance is mine sneer' break out on my kisser. "I have several. What are your favorites?"

I think I saw Tucker do an eye roll. He didn't seem to be the *'gun guy'* that Dedd is, and of course, like I am. He seems to be more of a luxury and fashion guy, which explains his affection for the Colt Diamondback. Luxury brand name, vintage weapon, looks nice in a hand that is sporting a Rolex Submariner on its wrist… that would be the Joe Tucker weapons selection criteria.

Johnny got my mind back on track about the rifle scopes as he explained his favorites. "I use Lucid Optics on my Remington 700."

"M24?"

"Duh."

"Of course, please continue."

"Anyway, a friend owns the company that makes those. But I also like Burris. They make good stuff. I've been thinking about scoring a Leatherwood Camputer though.. That whole adjustable ranging telescope thing has me intrigued."

His enthusiasm for the tools of long-range shots was contagious. But like they say, ask ten gun enthusiasts about an optic and you'll get fifteen answers. It was my turn to go up to bat. "I have a Nightforce on my Fifty," I announced grandly.

I could hear Dedd getting a boner, which I found disturbing.

I continued, "But I also have a Leopold, A US Optics FDN 25, and a Steiner."

Dedd smiled, "Of course the Steiner goes without saying. I have one too."

The conversation could have gone on all night, but I knew we needed to cut it short. I felt like I finally bonded with Johnny Dedd. "Let me go get the Barrett." I excused myself and went upstairs.

When I returned from my visit to the gun vault, I could see the combination of glee and awe in Dedd's eyes. Even Tucker was appreciative of my firearms art masterpiece.

I held it out like a father showing off his first newborn. That is, if a father held a baby like a big honking thirty-pound rifle. "Gentlemen, I present the Barrett 50BMG caliber rifle. The

M107A1 with a twenty-nine-inch fluted barrel weighing in at just a biscuit under twenty-nine pounds."

The slight scent of Hoppe's Number 9 and freedom wafted through the room.

Dedd actually stood up as if the Pope had just wandered into the joint. He's a good Catholic... not Dedd, but the Pope, at least the one we *used* to have... John Paul. I don't care much for the new guy. Maybe Dedd is a good Catholic too. I don't really know. As for me, not a great Catholic.

"Holy shit," Dedd muttered inelegantly, as he took in the view.

Speaking of taking in the view, even Tucker's face resembled a midwestern tourist's initial gaze into the vastness of the Grand Canyon.

After a respectful moment of reflection on the two-thousand-meter-plus official cause of death for so many terrorists and commies, Johnny Dedd summarized nicely." That ought to get the job done, Becker. Let's do this shit."

"Then we have a plan. Next stop is the Miami River waterfront."

CHAPTER 9

My bullet-resistant vest felt snug enough. My body fat index probably gave me more *'resistance to lead poisoning'* than the material they make these things out of. I had no doubt at least one shot would be fired in anger in the next thirty seconds.

Dedd was perched on a rooftop across the street. His presence provided little or no help unless we brought the fight back outside. Still, having a sniper outside for backup always provides a sense of well-being. We probably wouldn't be outside because this time our plan consisted of breaching the door, throwing everyone present down on their faces, and kicking some ass. Our leverage was surprise. I don't think they expected us to come back and kill them so fast after the little raid they staged at my place.

"You ready, Tucker?" I asked.

"Sure… let's rock."

I didn't want to rock… I just wanted to kill the guy who ordered my home to be invaded.

It was time.

I booted the door, and it went down like a bulldozer hit it. I still pack a mean kick, even at my age, and my size eleven triple wides will get the job done.

I button-hooked left, Tucker followed me in and button-hooked right.

"Hey assholes, up against the wall!" I hadn't used that phrase since I was a cop. It felt good. I might have even gotten a little teary-eyed. As you get older, your control over your emotions diminishes somewhat. With my gun in my mitt, a broken door, and assholes up against the wall, I was almost overcome with nostalgia.

Inside, we were surprised to find there were only two assholes present. They did get up against the wall as requested, and they did it quickly.

I like cooperation.

These two seem to be cooperative types, at least when they have automatic weapons screwed in their ears. Although, the tall one was starting to get a bit pissy. Tucker gave him a love tap to the kidneys to settle him down.

The other prisoner was a short, skinny, hillbilly looking grub with long unkempt red hair. The tall pissy one looked like some crazy-eyed, scraggly bearded pervert radical.

I ran cover while Joe frisked them. Then he zipped tied their hands and ankles and placed them face down on the floor, side by side. I saw two semi-auto pistols come off their bodies and get stuffed into Tucker's belt. We cleared all the other rooms and the docks. No one else was present.

After we took control of the building, Tucker texted Dedd one word... clear.

I decided to conduct an interrogation at the scene rather than trying to move these two. I applied all the training technique and finesse I acquired during my two-plus decades of law enforcement.

"Hey shit-bag, are you some kind of a terrorist or something?" I asked.

The guy I was speaking to angrily grunted something in what sounded like Arabic. I took that as a firm 'maybe.'

I addressed the other guy. "What's your story?"

'I'm an asshole."

"I can see that. Who are you working for?"

"Boris. He hires guys like me to work on his projects. Usually foreigners, but I applied and got a job."

"No shit? You had to apply to be an asshole?"

"Yeah, I had to bring my arrest records, show them my prison tattoos, find a couple of references I pulled jobs with. It was harder than getting a restaurant job. But with my strong prison record, I got in."

He described his criminal history like academics blather on about their degrees and published papers. I had to respect the man's pride in his professional achievements.

"So, what about the terrorists?" Tucker asked.

"That's a different thing. This dick here is a fucking terrorist." He wiggled his nose towards the other turd-waffle we had tied up on the floor.

"Does he speak English?" Tucker asked.

"Not enough. Plus, he is always whacking it... before a job, after a job, during a job... just jabbering away in whatever the hell language he speaks and wanking. It's all he ever does. I can't stand that piece of shit. If you are going to kill us, kill him first so I can watch. I'd like to see that prick get wasted before I die."

Tucker and I stepped back for a quickly whispered conference.

"Joe, I think we have a disgruntled employee here."

"I agree. He doesn't seem happy with the direction his career is going."

"I don't blame him. Would you be happy if you were left on guard duty with a fucking terrorist?"

"No... I can't say that would be ideal. Especially one who spanks the monkey all the time... which is weird." Joe said.

"The terrorist seems hostile... can't speak much English. I don't think we need him."

"Yeah, he is definitely a liability. But I think we can work with this other guy. I can see him being a lot of help. He knows the players *and* the plan."

"That works for me. We can use him... the other guy, not so much."

"Do it."

Joe texted a quick message to Johnny... *'come in.'*

A few minutes later, Dedd walked in carrying a big rifle in a rolled-up piece of carpet. Terrorist dude and asshole dude both got wide-eyed at the sight of him. Somehow, vicious animals know and recognize other vicious animals intuitively. I strongly suspect that Johnny is a functioning psychopath… on his good days. It shows. Our prisoners might agree.

I spoke next. "Johnny, we have one we don't need and one to interrogate. We'll leave it up to you as to how to proceed."

Asshole guy spouted off with more than a bit of desperation in his voice, "Remember! I'm on your side!"

Johnny only considered the situation for a brief moment before rolling the tall man over on his back with his foot. Then he meticulously pulled on a pair of surgical gloves, kneeled down, and slowly strangled terrorist dude with his bare hands, staring asshole guy in the eyes during the entire process. I believe he was sending a message. I also believed the message was received.

Johnny's barbarous deed was appalling to witness, I suppose because cold blooded murder can be appalling to watch in many cases. But this recently deceased scumbag was a member of the crew who attacked my home. You come after me at my home, I turn loose the animal within, or in this case, the animal without, meaning Johnny Deddario. Could I have done it? I'm not a psychopath like my colleague, but every man has the potential to murder. It simply requires the proper stimulus. If my wife had been alive when my home was attacked. I'd have absolutely strangled this piece of shit myself.

The asshole guy peed himself.

When the terrorist guy stopped twitching, Johnny released his hands from the dead man's throat and began his interrogation of the subject we now lovingly refer to as asshole guy. "Tell them the parts you left out, please."

Asshole guy couldn't talk fast enough. He went full motor mouth to the point of being unintelligible.

"Slow down, asshole," Tucker said, as he tried to take some

notes. "Take a deep breath, then start from the beginning."

He did as instructed and began again."My name is Potter... my friends call me Worm."

"Like Rodman?" I asked.

"Who?"

I guess he's not an old-time basketball fan. "Never mind, Worm. Spill it," I ordered.

Worm took another deep breath, gulped, and tried again. "Okay, so, I work for that dirtbag, Boris. Do you know him?"

"We've heard of him," Johnny said. "Do you know what he looks like?"

"Sure."

"So, what does he look like?" I asked, growing impatient with Worm's drifting thought process.

"Big guy, maybe late forties, tall, beefy, with black hair, has some gold frame glasses, wears a leather jacket... stupid accent, kind of an asshole."

The description was pretty good. I'd recognize him anywhere.

"Go on," I said.

"Anyway, Boris, he's a real prick. I'll be honest with you. I hate his guts. He treats me like shit. Boris hates Americans, which is a dick attitude, but he needs English speakers who blend in... So, like I said, he hates me, but I'm good at my job and that keeps me employed."

"What all do you do for him?" I asked.

"Oh, I been doing some English speaking, like I mentioned... some bagman shit, some occasional rough stuff, moving around women, money, drugs... you know, business stuff. But I promise you, I'm done with all that shit now. I'm going to get an honest job after this. Mister Dedd showed me the light."

"Okay. Keep going. Tell us what Boris is doing here."

"Well, other than terrorist shit, he ran a scam on some rich dicks on the west coast. Only the middleman in the deal stole the take... or he did something with it and they killed him for it, which was stupid. Now nobody knows where the money went. And now we have some crazy Russian guy from California running around killing people trying to get to Boris."

"What about the terrorists?" Johnny asked coldly.

I could see a visible change in Worm when Johnny spoke. He instantly morphed from cooperating individual to a terrified potential murder victim.

Worm sputtered at me, "Don't let *him* kill me. You do it... Make it fast please... a bullet in the back of the head. I deserve at least that, don't I?"

I tried to calm him down. "Don't worry, Worm... just keep talking and this will work out fine. Now answer my colleague here... what about the terrorists?"

"He brought over about fifty of them. They're scary assholes... maybe Al Qaida guys... or some other assholes... ISIS... did you ever hear of ISIS? They're supposed to be assholes. Anyway, he has them housed in some old factory building right now, but they are going back to the freighter tonight to pick up the bomb, then they're going to blow up South Beach."

"Bomb?"

"Yeah, it's a little nuke or something. They are going to make a big scene with a shoot-out and hostages, then detonate the bomb."

"Why?"

"To piss people off, I think."

"So, you aren't in on the end game plan?"

"I think that *is* the end game plan. These guys aren't geniuses, sir. They're terrorists. Boris was hired to help them and I got hired by Boris, which turned out to be a shit stick of a deal."

I felt that was a pretty profound statement coming from Worm. I took a moment to ponder on what a shit stick was though.

Dedd asked, "Where is Boris now?"

"He's with his guys picking up the terrorists to go stage on the freighter. He stole a school bus to shuttle them back."

Dedd stayed on point. "How many of his own men does he have?"

"Maybe twenty or twenty-five guys, plus those fifty terrorist bastards, after he picks them up. So, under a hundred."

"You are pretty good at math, Worm," Johnny said, clearly impressed with his prisoner's calculations.

"Thank you. I learned my all my numbers and words good. I went completely through to seventh grade," he stated proudly, as if he completed a doctorate in doctoral stuff.

I got him back on track. "What vehicles do they have?" I asked.

"Three black SUVs, I think... maybe four... They'll be running cover for the bus."

"Any idea where the take is from the California scam?"

"No... but Boris is going to try to find it, if that scary Russian guy doesn't get it first."

"Who knows where the money is?"

"Just that Schuster guy knew. And maybe that old cougar-gold digger woman. I think she knows more than she's saying."

"Shit."

"Yeah." Then Potter threw a curve ball into the conversation. "But Mister Boss, Boris isn't the one I'd be worried about."

Johnny interjected himself into my interrogation, "He's not the boss, Worm. If anybody is the boss, it's probably me, but we don't operate with a boss."

I gave Johnny the look of a man who had to listen to unrequested bullshit. "Johnny, just let him talk."

"Fine." Johnny sulked a little.

I tried again to question Worm. "Call me Becker. And who is it we *should* be worried about?"

"Kruger. He's a real piece of work. Big son of a bitch, too. Big old German looking guy. Big muscles, fat head, scary blue eyes."

"So, he is actually a real guy and he's here?"

"I don't know if Kruger is his real name but he's the head guy,"

Worm insisted.

"No shit?"

"Yeah, he's the worst of the bunch... and coming from me, that makes him pretty bad."

"What's his story?" I asked.

"He's in charge of everything. He's actually the boss of Boris and all the rest."

"Right. I get that... But where is he?"

"Miami."

"Why?"

"This forty-million-dollar score was a Boris thing. Boris screwed it up and lost the money. Kruger is following up. Maybe he will kill Boris, and I can go home."

"No."

"Okay."

Was Potter pouting?

I continued, "Does Kruger have any men with him?"

"Maybe ten. Nothing major."

I switched my line of questioning. "Do you think Kruger killed the middleman?"

Worm considered the query before answering. "That's his style," he intoned. "But it could have been Boris following orders too. Or maybe Boris gave the order. Or Boris did it himself."

"You're guessing aren't you, Worm."

"Now that you mention it, I think I am."

"You really don't know shit, when it comes right down to it, do you?"

"No... not really. I'd just like to get out of this alive."

"Fine. No more guessing, no making up stuff. You either know or you don't know. You have one job. I need you to identify these guys for Johnny. I'll handle the rest. If you see them and point them out to Johnny, many of your problems will be solved and perhaps even all your dreams will come true."

"Thanks, Becker. I like working for you."

"Just don't screw me over, Worm. I'll melt your face off with a blowtorch and let iguanas eat your brains."

Worm's eyes disclosed honest fear at the thought of local lizards eating his gray matter, not that it would make much of a meal. I think he is afraid of iguanas. I also think he's convinced there might be more than one violent psychopath on our team. In my opinion, as a professional, scaring the hell out of people keeps them in line. We scared the hell out of Mr. Worm.

I made a command decision. "Johnny, find some duct tape and make a mummy out of Worm. No need to kill him yet. We might need him again. Put him in the trunk of your car.'

Johnny had a quizzical look on his face. "No problem. But what about the terrorists?"

"They aren't our job," I said flatly.

"Yeah, but they're terrorists." Johnny spoke the words slowly and deliberately.

"Cops can fight them. Did you miss the part about a hundred guys and a bomb?"

"So?" Johnny threw me an icy stare that was as grim as a toothless man with a steak dinner in front of him.

"I see your point."

There comes a time when you know the need to kill terrorists outweighs the need to retain common sense. The street cops, detectives, and SWAT guys can certainly kill them all it if their bosses let them. But all it takes is one politically oriented pussy police executive to call in the FBI and the whole thing will get screwed up, and then innocent people will die pointlessly. The police are hindered by protocol, chain of command, and regulations. Regular Americans are not. We can do whatever it takes to get the job done. But we also had our actual job, finding the forty-million. And I needed to know why Schuster mentioned me in his cryptic note. That was the mission. Find the money, solve the puzzle. But still. Terrorists suck.

Tucker came up with at least part of the answer to our approach, if not the answer to our questions.

"The woman is the only legitimate key. She has to know. I say we grab her after we kill the terrorists and wrap this thing up. If she doesn't know, the money is in the wind."

It sounded like Tucker was already committed to whacking the terrorists.

I asked, "Will you get paid though, if we don't recover the funds?"

"Mister Stump will convince our client to pay for our time. We might not get the big percentage from a recovery fee, but we'll get a nice payday out of it."

"Fine. Let's do this then."

"Same plan?"

"Sure. A sniper, two-man hit team, and surprise on our side."

Worm spoke again, "Excuse me for saying... That doesn't sound like enough... I don't want to get left to die in the car trunk. Let me go with you. I can fight."

"You already had your ass kicked once. And you're an asshole."

"Exactly."

I couldn't argue with his logic. I couldn't fully comprehend it either. But it's been that kind of day.

Johnny surprised me with an intellectual comment.

"Worm, do you remember what Horatius said at the bridge when he faced the Etruscan invaders?"

Tucker and I both looked at each other in amazement... *where the hell did that come from?*

Worm said, "I know what a bridge is... that whole thing by the freighter is like a bridge... is the answer bridge?"

"No,, asshole... Horatius said, how can a man die better than facing fearful odds?"

"What the hell does that mean?"

"It means that if you come with us, you don't get a gun and you will probably die."

"I'd rather die fighting than get left in a car trunk in Florida if you all get killed. Did I tell you I was in the Army until they kicked me out? I hate terrorists. Especially that guy there who wanked all the time." He leaned over and spit on the corpse of deceased masturbation-enthusiast.

"Fine, you're in," I said. "You spot for Johnny. If you piss him off, it's your ass."

Worm appeared apprehensive about the offer. "Wait, he's already pissed off. When does that pissed off part start?"

"Okay, if you piss him off worse... then it's your ass."

"Fair enough. I'm in."

"Cut him loose, Johnny. But keep an eye on him."

Johnny flipped open a knife and cut the zip ties. Worm did a brisk rub on his wrists and ankles, then sat up with his back against the wall.

I whispered to Tucker, "Did that just happen?"

He whispered back, "That literary shit was from some poem Mister Stump told him about. He seemed to obsess with it. Don't worry, he's still a maniac. To be honest, I'm surprised he didn't quote a Bronco Hammer book."

"Me too. But it is unnerving to think that Johnny is the brains of that pair."

"I see your point. But we also just recruited that stupid asshole to the team."

"Who would you rather have on the team during something like this, a random asshole or a guy you would hate to see get killed?"

"True."

"Plus, a reformed asshole is like an American mutt. Loyal, obedient... makes a good cop...well, maybe not him, but if you get one young enough, they make good cops."

"Okay. Worm is in. We'll see how he works out."

"Johnny can always stomp his head flat. He gets a kick out of doing that. It's like bubble wrap to him."

I was a bit taken aback by his cavalier attitude about

gruesome murders. "What the fuck kind of people do you deal with in Los Angeles?"

"The usual." he shrugged.

"Oh." As a cop, I understood what he meant on a visceral level.

I turned and addressed Dedd and Worm. "Worm, find clean pants and skivvies. Then do whatever the hell Mister Dedd tells you to do and do it to the letter. If you screw up, you're a prime candidate for a dumpster funeral in the closest alley. And I promise you, Mister Dedd will never feel any compassion for you no matter what you say or do."

"No problem. Sorry I pissed myself, sir. Shit happens... or piss happens... one of those. I got a change of clothes here. I'll clean up and get to work."

Worm wandered off to square himself away, with Johnny supervising his activity.

As Worm and Dedd went into a room in the back, I asked Joe a pertinent question. "Tucker, do you think Worm will discover a cure for heart disease or maybe calculate the grand unification theory?"

Tucker snickered, "He barely has a cure for pissing his pants. But he'll do... I'll be honest, Becker, he might be a piece of shit, but he grows on you."

"True. Can't hold that against him, though. I guess at one point or another, we're all a piece of shit in somebody's world."

"Pretty sure Worm is a piece of shit in everybody's world. But now it looks like he's *our* piece of shit, so... there's that."

"Wisdom."

There wasn't much left to say about Worm and his worm brain, so Tucker got back down to business. "Alright, Becker. Let's figure out how we take down a hundred guys and not get arrested."

There would be arrangements to be made and surprises to prepare.

We found a table and went to work.

CHAPTER 10

The plan was simple. Find the bad guys and shoot all of them... of course, there *were* certain refinements included in this course of action.

Refinement one, engage them at the Port Boulevard Bridge before they could get to the port island and their boat.

Refinement two, set up a distraction for the local Miami police officers.

Refinement three, set up a distraction for the Port Authority officers.

And finally, refinement four, kill everybody and escape.

Boris's cargo vessel was docked in the Port of Miami, a location connected to the city with bridges spanning the Biscayne Bay from downtown. The bad guys would be rolling in with their motorcade from downtown Miami, crossing the bridge onto the port, making a stop at their boat, then moving on through the tunnels up and around to the Miami Beach tourist area known as South Beach. There they would wreak havoc and detonate their ordinance, or as we laypersons call it, their effen nuke.

Our job was to stop them on the bridge, prevent access to their boat and Miami Beach, and then figure out how to stop the bomb from going off. The more I reflect on this plan, the more I suspect we should have brought another seven-hundred guys with us.

The clock was ticking, but we had enough time to get set up. Johnny and Worm were on high ground in the sniper position, with Worm assigned to point out Boris and Kruger, ideally to take as prisoners for questioning, but as a last resort to be prime sniper targets for the fifty caliber. Although that *last resort* part wasn't written in stone. Tucker and I would face the rest of them *'head on'* at the entrance to the port coming out of downtown Miami.

There were key elements to the plan's success, like capture Kruger or Boris and try to torture… I mean question… them regarding the location of the forty-million dollars. And how to defuse the bomb, of course… but mostly we wanted to recover the forty million.

The down sides were simple. If the caravan got past us, it was a straight shot to South Beach where they would slaughter hundreds of locals and tourists before eventually detonating their bomb. Oh, there would be the typical protracted negotiations with the police, so the news could film it for the entertainment of their terrorist buddies back home, but the fate of South Beach was already decided. It was our job to un-decide it.

Obviously, there were many loose ends to our plan, but none of us were particularly detail oriented individuals… Tucker was the closest thing we had to a quality assurance manager. I base that solely on how well he searched that warehouse when we first started working together, and of course, some of his more stable ideas. Although most ideas normal people put forth seem stable when compared to Johnny Dedd's ideas.

Still, it was time for an old man to go once more into the breech. I didn't have anywhere else to be.

It was almost midnight and traffic was light, as most weeknights can be. I saw them coming. A bus and three black SUVs. I hoped Boris and Kruger were in this motorcade.

I looked at Tucker and said the word he had been waiting for. "Now."

He retrieved a small electronic device from his pocket and detonated a car bomb on top of an abandoned parking garage in North Beach. That should send the cops on the Miami Beach side scrambling north out of our area and hopefully allowing us to escape after we save the day.

I gave another command. "Make the calls, Johnny."

Dedd made three quick calls from a burner phone. One reported the car bomb we just lit up as a terrorist attack. The other call was the report of an imminent bomb detonation on one of the cruise ships on the other island in the Port, which would effectively shut down traffic on the other bridge for a while. The last was a false report of a sniper in Overton. That should keep downtown Miami officers out of our hair.

Our goal was to keep the cops busy... and alive... and also, having them tied up with stuff that does not involve arresting us.

The convoy closed on our position. Tucker and I stepped out on the bridge. We each had M4s with hundred round drum magazines.

I sent a message to Dedd via my comm unit. "Take them now."

The roar of the fifty caliber rifle was deep and loud over the water. A massive round hit the engine block of the lead vehicle. The next round ripped apart the left front tire of the bus. The third round killed the bus driver. The fourth and fifth took out the rest of the motorcade vehicles.

Then it got weird.

Instead of turning around, surrendering, quitting... or something reasonable, all the terrorists and their escorts bailed out of the damaged vehicles and charged like they were extras in Braveheart.

Now, to the typical layperson, the hypothetical individual I previously mentioned, a hundred rampaging terrorists with guns might not sound like a *lot* of terrorists, but when you are half of the only two guys facing them, they definitely look like a *whole* lot of terrorists

Most of them carried either AK47s or M4s like us. They didn't seem happy. They were closing fast from less than two hundred yards away.

How do I get myself involved in this shit?

We walked out on the bridge towards them. "Stand fast, Johnny. We hit them at a hundred yards. Kill them when they're tired."

"Copy that."

From his perch, Dedd sustained fire on the vehicles while worm searched the mob for signs of Boris or Kruger with field glasses. I could hear them over the comm units we had plugged in our ears.

"I don't see them them, Mister Dedd," Worm whined.

"Keep looking. They have to be there."

The rush of bad guys crossed the hundred yard point of demarcation.

I shouted, "Let 'em have it, Tucker."

We opened up with hundred round mag-dumps, spraying the oncoming mob with sustained fire and advanced on them. Dedd continued to deliver death from above.

They returned fire, which forced us to the sides of the bridge by the pedestrian walkways, which provided not much cover, but at least we weren't standing in the middle of the road.

They did the same.

This turn of events was good, from my perspective. Rather than a wall of bad guys, there were now two lines of bad guys who couldn't all get a sight picture on us at the same time, although enough did get a sight picture to be awkward.

It became apparent that our plan sucked, and we were going to get overrun and killed. But then something weird happened. I'm still uncertain if it is good or bad weird, but definitely weird.

A great big bastard with a belt-fed machine gun came behind us, not shooting us, but spraying down our terrorist visitors while laughing his ass off.

The size of the guy was inhuman. He was like a gigantic bear, with long white hair, a grizzly white beard, and a long black coat.

That was not what I was expecting to see today.

He wiped out about a dozen of Boris's men instantly before flopping prone on the ground and continuing to fire.

I wondered if I was hallucinating. I wondered where a giant with a belt-fed machine gun came from. I wondered why I got myself into this situation and let it escalate out of control like this.

I thought about this and other things as I became a leaf on the wind, as that one guy said in a television show I used to watch.

Being completely weightless was not what I had in mind for my future weight loss plan. But then, let's face it, in the heat of battle, sometimes mistakes are made. It's no one's fault really. Sometimes things just happen unexpectedly. Like one of Johnny's rounds hitting a car, and the bomb that was meant for South Beach going off on the bridge instead.

It wasn't a nuke, fortunately, but it felt like one.

Amazingly, I wasn't killed. Nevertheless, we blew up the bridge, which is embarrassing. All the bad guys were vaporized. That part was nice, but even so, you can't accidently destroy major infrastructure without someone getting yelled at.

As the concussion knocked me off the side railings into the water below, I swear I heard Dedd say *that was cool*, in my ear comm unit.

Well, shit happens.

I splashed down hard into the salty Biscayne Bay, but was otherwise unscathed. In the Bible, they call that a miracle. I call it a miracle too. I made it back to the surface, puked up some salt water, swam to the shoreline, climbed over some rocks, and made my way back up to the road.

I didn't have cheering throngs of people awaiting me, grateful that I saved South Beach and survived the fall. But I *did* have a couple of assholes willing to help me get the hell out of there, and that was good enough.

Dedd and Worm grabbed me by the arms and rushed me to the car. Tucker was already behind the wheel.

"I'd give that dive an 8.7, Becker," Tucker laughed as we hauled ass out of the Port.

I didn't think his joke was that funny.

Dedd snickered.

Worm kept his mouth shut.

Worm isn't as stupid as I thought.

"Did you see Boris or Kruger?" I asked.

"Not a sign of them," Worm said bitterly. "Sorry, boys. I hope you don't kill me."

We ignored Worm's whining.

"Did anyone see that guy with the machine gun?"

"I thought he was with you?" Dedd said casually, as if he was used to situations involving terrorists and giants with belt-fed machine guns.

"Where'd he go?"

"I don't know. I didn't see him after the explosion," Tucker said.

Tucker was a pretty good driver. He flew across the port, accessed the tunnel under the bay, and in a few minutes were heading back into town on the MacArthur Causeway.

"That was some high-speed shit, Tucker," I said as I got the nerve to let a breath out.

"I was a driving instructor at the police department back in the day."

"Me too," Dedd muttered. "I'd have gotten us out on the bridge."

"What bridge?" I asked.

"The one from the Port to Miami Beach."

"There isn't one."

"Oh…. never mind."

Tucker piped up, "Wasn't there something in the plan about disarming the bomb rather than detonating the bomb?"

"Yeah, we didn't make it to that part," I said.

"So, are we going to need a new plan?"

"I believe so, yes. We still don't know where Boris is. We don't know where Krueger is. And we don't know where the forty-million is."

"But the terrorists are dead," Johnny grumbled. "That's a good thing."

"Yeah... that wasn't why we were here, though. And now, we got to make sure we don't get our names attached to blowing up a major fucking bridge." I might have said that a little louder and angrier than I meant to.

Worm spoke out, "Terrorists blew that up. Totally not our fault. Besides, it's better than blowing up South Beach, right?"

I was impressed with his perspective. Worm was growing on me.

"Yeah, I guess so... Let's get back to my place and regroup. This isn't how I saw the day going."

Tucker agreed. "Me neither, but you have to admit, it was cool."

I didn't respond.

But it was definitely cool.

CHAPTER 11

I grabbed beers out of the refrigerator and distributed them to the team, plus Worm, as we gathered around my dining room table.

"The news is reporting a tanker truck of gasoline exploded at the bridge. No mention of shooting or terrorists," Johnny announced.

"Typical. They cover up shit when it doesn't need covered up."

"They're calling it an environmental issue and the announcer said something about electric cars and no gas... are they stupid or what?"

"Yeah, they're stupid. Everything gets a political spin and nothing true ever gets told... that's the state of the nation, boys," Worm pontificated as he took a long drag on his beer.

Dedd addressed his next words to Worm. "You know, killing you isn't off the table yet. So, you might not want to make yourself too comfortable, bub."

A pounding knock at the door startled us all into action. It was kind of cool really. Dedd and Tucker exited the open patio doors, each button-hooking to opposite sides and probably flanking whoever was banging on my door. At the same time, Worm chugged his beer in one gulp, flipped the bottle like a baton in his hand, ready to use as a war club. He followed me to the entrance, taking a position on the opposite side of the door frame from me.

"Who is it?" I yelled.

A deep voice answered in broken English with a heavy Russian accent. "Not enemy... Is Igor... I am here to be the talk. I swear I not kill you for one hour."

I opened the door to find the guy with the belt-fed machine gun filling my entranceway with his massive bulk. Dedd and Tucker were at tactical angles behind him with guns pointed at the big Russian from California.

"Want a beer?" I asked.

"You have Vodka, yes?" he answered with his own question.

"I have vodka, yes. Come in and sit down."

I assessed the situation and determined two things. One, this guy could kill us all if he wanted to and we probably couldn't kill him back. And two, it looked like this was going to be one of those times when you have to pow-wow with a giant commie and drink heavily.

As we all cautiously settled around the table with our drinks, Dedd asked a blunt question before I could stop him.

"Are you Russian mob?"

Igor didn't appear fazed by the inquiry. "Not mob... something else."

Johnny didn't quit. "What's the deal with Eagle Rock, Igor?

Igor's face hardened. He paused an uncomfortably long moment before continuing. "We do not speak of this thing. It is unwise to do so. But I can tell you I was one who went to John Christianson and helped him with that case. I can't tolerate children being kidnapped. Those men were the scum. Embarrassment to my country. Is what you call it... rude?"

Dedd nodded, satisfied with the answer. "Yeah. It is rude. I'd have done the same thing."

Igor continued, "I am here to get money back and kill people who rip off Igor. You work on case. I pay you, not kill you. I help now."

His accent was heavy and his mastery of the English language was rougher than a dried up starfish, but I understood the man and his intentions. "Fine. You are part of the team. This is Tucker, Dedd, and Worm. I'm Becker."

"I know you all. I was Spetsnaz and KGB when younger... I

still have connections. Can find out things. But can't find my money. I need you. Not kill you."

Tucker replied, "I appreciate you not killing us. But we are already working for a client to recover those funds."

Igor was undeterred. "You not understand. When I return to California, I will rip off client's head and shit down neck. He is idiot. I pay you double. You work for me now."

I noticed Igor seemed to be getting worked up, so I pulled a King Solomon and saved the day. "They have a client. My client is dead. I'll be *your* investigator. They'll continue to serve their client, if you agree not to kill him... We all work together. Okay, yes?"

Shit, now I am talking like him.

Igor's face cracked with what might have been either a smile or a sneer. "It is okay, yes... this will be arrangement," Igor stated, closing the deal. "But your client is still on Igor's shit list."

"Deal?" I posed the question to my two California colleagues.

Dedd and Tucker looked at each other before Tucker spoke for the pair. "Deal."

I closed the negotiation portion of our discussion. "Then it's settled."

Dedd got the operation back on track. "We need to decide what approach we take to recovering the money. I think the woman is too dangerous."

Tucker added, "And I think Boris and Kruger are going to want to reckon accounts with us."

Igor frowned. "Kruger is bad news. He needs to die."

"You know him?" I asked.

"No... I know of him. He is the trouble. Kruger set up terror attack. Kruger set up rip off on fake gold bars. Kruger is brain. Must cut out brain."

"Do you think he knows where the money is?" Dedd asked.

"No... only woman knows... maybe she does not know either. Schuster was fool to trust her."

"Faraday?"

"Yes, the gold digging whore."

"That's her reputation," Tucker added.

"But where is she?" Johnny asked.

I answered. "I have a pal who runs a diner on the pier. He knows a network of her victims, former paramours, whatever. Anyway, he can call some of them and find her. We just need to figure out how to stay away from Boris and Kruger."

"Leave to me," Igor stated. "I will have throwing party at Mike's Brewery in Miami tonight. Will invite them."

"You mean you are throwing a party?" Worm asked.

"Whatever. Be there at nine. You see. We don't find them. Let them find us."

The Pub - Ninth Floor

I wasn't sure what was going on with this operation, but our luck had not been great with Boris and Kruger. They had men attack my home and try to attack South Beach. We stopped them but we hadn't faced them down yet. My best guess was they still had at least ten of their best goons with them. It didn't seem like the ideal time to sit at a rooftop pub drinking. Igor didn't see it that way, though.

"Drink.. enjoy. This is on Igor," the big Russian said loudly as we chilled out on the deck looking at the view of downtown, probably awaiting certain death.

The air was moving at that altitude and provided some pleasant relief from the street level heat.

"What makes you think they will show up?" Johnny asked as he took a sip from his Manhattan.

"Word is out. I killed their men. Word is out. I will be here."

"Who told? Who put the word out?" Tucker asked.

"I did. Through Russian contacts. Now everyone in Miami knows Igor is here."

"Why does this seem like a bad idea?" I said, putting the

question out there.

"Because it is bad idea... bad idea for Boris and Kruger," Igor said before bursting into peals of raucous laughter.

We laughed along uncomfortably. That was right before the evening took an unusual turn.

It seems the pub has three access points, two sets of stairs and an elevator. Armed men poured out of each of them.

We were outside on the patio by the pool. There wasn't a lot of cover. Things were not looking promising.

Oddly, Igor was still laughing.

I reached for my Sig.

The lights went out before I could break leather. Someone unplugged the entire joint. Other than starlight and the ambient light of the city, we were in complete darkness.

"What the hell is going on?" Tucker asked.

"My guys work in kitchen and in maintenance. They help me set up what you call the ambush."

"This is not how ambushes work, Igor," Dedd grouched. "You don't set yourself up in a pocket to get overrun by superior numbers."

"Today we do, da?" Will be fine."

People were screaming and running towards exits. Some kind of heavily armed bad guy ninjas we sweeping the place with automatic weapons.

I'm definitely posting a Yelp review on this shit.

The guys flipped the table over and drew weapons. This was not ideal.

Smoke!

Fire?

Smoke grenades. Who threw them? The Boris and Kruger gang or...

It was Igor. He was tossing smoke grenades. At least we had a slight chance to use the confusion to attempt escape.

A massive paw wrapped around my head forcing me to look

nose to nose with Igor. Evidently, he wanted to speak with me.

"Dis is the good, da?" he growled merrily.

"No Da! No Da, Igor... they outnumber and outgun us. We have to make a break for it."

A burst of automatic weapons fire hit the pool water splashing us. Tucker and Dedd were returning fire. Dedd seemed to be in his happy place.

Igor laughed at my concern. "I lure them out, like animals. We have Boris and Kruger now. I'll have talk with them."

"What?" I was confused, but Igor pushed me aside to his left and stood up.

I began seeking targets and an exit, not necessarily in that order.

My last glimpse to my right I saw Igor pull something ungodly out from under his sport coat. He is a beast of a man, otherwise the weapon would have been impossible to conceal. I've read about the ShAK-12 bullpup urban combat weapon, but I've never seen one. And I've never heard of one with a compact anti-personnel grenade launcher attached to it. Yet, here it is.

Igor marched into the mayhem, slaughtering the attackers like it was Christmas in Chicago. It was a sight to behold. I was inspired enough to do something stupid and join him. At my age, getting killed on a Miami high-rise rooftop shooting it out with extreme criminal assholes seemed a lot better than a slow death in a nursing home... when the adrenalin pumps through your central nervous system like a horny poodle on your ankle, you get crazy thoughts like that.

We counter-attacked. All of us. Even Worm rolled with us holding a beer bottle in each hand.

It appeared the bad guys didn't plan on resistance.

I heard Worm shout, "Boris is here. He's over there."

He pointed wildly at the man we were hunting for, or the man who was hunting us, depending on your perspective.

Bullets hit all around us. Subsonic and suppressed, as best I could tell.

I saw a panicking young woman jump up and run into the intense fire. Worm leaped over a chair and pushed her out of the way. It was a selfless hero type move.

Worm absorbed a couple of rounds and went down.

I'd like to say, he'll be difficult to replace, but...

Igor smashed through the crowd, laughing and firing. He spotted four of the attackers stacking by each side of a door, preparing to flank us. He launched a grenade from his rifle, killing the pack of them instantly, but also starting a small fire by the elevators.

I worked my way through the bar enjoying my first wild west saloon shoot-out. One of the busboys, a little Cuban dude, hopped over a table and launched a kung fu sidekick into a pair of bad guys working their way along the booths inside. I used that as an opportunity to stand over their sprawled bodies and shoot them both in the face. Little Cuban dude gave me a high-five.

"Get your ass down, man. These are professionals," I warned.

"Nobody pulls this shit in Miami, my friend," he said in a surprisingly deep voice. He sounded like that interesting man who sold beer in commercials. Especially the 'my friend' part.

"Get one of their weapons and get your staff to safety. We'll handle these assholes."

"Are you cops?"

"Ehhh... not so much."

"Good, that's better. I'll get our servers out of here. Good job, man."

I zigged right and my new Cuban buddy zigged left. There were still plenty of targets remaining, unfortunately.

I saw Igor, Dedd, and Tucker moving like a well-tuned SWAT team as they advanced through the crowd. In less than thirty seconds, the weapon fire subsided. The attackers were down. There were only ten of them. It seemed like more.

"Becker!"

I heard the shout but couldn't tell if it was Tucker or Dedd. I cautiously moved in that direction.

I found them both gathered around a prone figure with a monster sitting on it. It was Boris. He was not looking fit as a fiddle, not even close.

Igor was on top of him, asking some pertinent questions.

"Where is money?"

Boris said something that was difficult to understand. It appeared as though speaking with a broken jaw and a bullet in your gut is difficult. Who knew?

Igor punched him in the aforementioned broken jaw.

Boris twitched and spasmed like it hurt. It certainly looked like it would hurt.

As best as I could tell, Boris told Igor something. I couldn't make out what it was. I could tell from their facial expressions that Tucker and Dedd couldn't hear it either. Whatever it was made Igor laugh... Igor seems to laugh a lot. He's pretty merry for a giant Russian assassin, or whatever the hell he is.

Igor looked at us with a wicked grin. "I have lead."

"Good. Let's get the hell out of here before the cops arrive."

"No, no, no!" Igor argued. "Not until we have throwing party I promised."

"You said you were *throwing* a party. I'd say you threw a pretty damned delightful party so far, Igor," Dedd answered.

"You do not understand plain English... I said throwing party. I meant throwing party."

With that declaration, he grabbed Boris by the foot and dragged him to the edge of the ninth floor deck and threw him off.

As the severely wounded Boris screamed all the way down to the street, Igor explained, "See? Throwing party. Boris got party. All good. Now let's get out of here."

I heard shuffling behind me. It was Worm.

"I thought you were dead, Worm?" I asked as I looked him over. He'd been shot a couple of times, but they looked to be either flesh wounds or through-and-throughs. If nothing vital was damaged, he might live.

"I got shot some, and I apologize for that, but I'll be fine."

I noticed he self-patched his wounds with some bar rags and seemed to be good to go. "You did fine Worm. Now let's get the hell out of here."

Igor talked as he led the way. "My men clean this up. No problem. All cameras are off and we have way out. Follow me."

We followed him. It wasn't like there were any other options. And he was the only one with a legitimate workable lead on the case now.

Four minutes later, we were in our cars and on the street, heading for my house. I sorted the case status in my head as we drove north.

Boris is gone.

Kruger is still out there someplace.

Faraday is probably in the wind.

Our only lead is held by a giant Russian psycho, who seems to be on our side.

And that's about it.

All in all, I can't say I'll miss Boris.

CHAPTER 12

Becker Residence - Lauderdale By The Sea

" Spill it, Igor. What did Boris tell you?" I was about done playing around with this Russian behemoth. He was either crazy or nuts, I couldn't decide which. But he had information we needed. It was time to close this case.

"Boris tell me important thing. Becker has the message. Woman will know how to find money with message."

"What?" I didn't get it. How did they know about the message? It must have been the torture session. We just found it before they did.

Dedd interjected, "Becker, get that message out and let's take another look. We must've missed something."

"I feel like we missed *everything*, Johnny. None of this makes any sense." I was puzzled. I went to the cabinet and retrieved my notebook. I keep copious notes daily in a small leather field notes folio. I usually write a few things in the morning and then summarize the day at night. It's a routine. I keep the archived notes in my safe, not that they are secret, but it's pretty much my life in there. I *did* make note of the strange message from Schuster. The original document went to my bank lock box, just in case. I transcribed the words with a black Sharpie to an eight by eleven sheet of printing paper and brought it down.

"Here it is. I can't make heads or tails out of it."

Worm, who wasn't hurt as badly as I thought, Tucker, Dedd, and Igor, peered over the page.

If I am found dead by suspicious circumstances, call Becker and tell him it was those guys from California. He will find them. Take in Grande, get to Pas.'

I stated what I felt was the obvious. "This is just some random scribbling. It doesn't make sense."

"Guys from California? Other than you and Worm, we are all from California," Dedd observed.

"Igor from Russia. Only live in California."

Worm said, "I'm from Eastern Kentucky."

"Is that different from Western Kentucky?" Tucker asked.

"Not much. But some."

Tucker replied, "I don't think you are a suspect, Worm. But keep thinking."

I put the conversation on pause with a raised hand. "Give me a minute. I want to check in with a guy."

I left the others to pontificate over the obscure clue while I retreated to my private office to phone the computer guru, Dourdhoff Jenkins.

"Jenkins."

"Dourdhoff, it's Becker."

"I know. I have you tracked to your house. Upstairs… must be your office."

"No, I'm in a phone booth in Detroit."

"Well, your phone is in your office at your home."

"Fine… just quit creeping on me. I need some help."

"I'm not creeping…exactly. Did you know Maggie drove by your house about four times in the past week? You should ask her out."

"How do you know this shit?

"I know what everybody does if they're tethered to a phone."

You *are* creeping… just stop and listen."

"Fine. What do you want?"

"I have a list of people involved in a case. I want to know if there is a California nexus for any of them."

"Send it."

I quickly cut and pasted the names into an email and sent it to him. I had the information in a word document for my case file already, so it only took a few seconds.

"Now I have a favor to ask." Dourdhoff said,

"What is it?"

"I'm buying an AP Royal Oak Grand Complication in rose gold on Monday from some guy I haven't dealt with before. Can you come along? I don't want to get robbed or pick up a counterfeit. It's close to seven-hundred-thousand bucks."

"Fine. I'd like to see it anyway. Where's the deal?"

"Jewelry store in Lauderdale-by-the-Sea. It's a friend of the owner. We're meeting inside. I'll send you all the information."

"Do you have your own watchmaker coming?"

"Of course."

"Fine. When can I get my list?"

"It's on its way back to you now."

"That was fast."

"It might seem that way to a Luddite."

"Blow it out your ass, Dourdhoff... and thank you!"

I disconnected, printed the information, quickly looked up what Luddite meant while I waited for the hard copies, cussed when I figured out what a Luddite is, then returned to the others.

I tossed the printout on the table. "Something interesting here. Check it out."

The group huddled and looked it over.

Dedd was the first to comment. "Since when is a big German-looking asshole terrorist international con-artist named Kruger from Torrance, California? I can see him being from the valley, but... wow."

Tucker chimed in, "He's a local asshole. For us... I mean... shit he went to Torrance High School, that's where they filmed Buffy!"

Igor, Worm and I all spoke at the same time. "Who?"

Tucker sounded defensive. "It was a popular TV show. I never watched it."

"So could he be the California guy who Schuster was talking about?" I asked.

Tucker answered. "Very possible. Schuster had California connections. He might have known Kruger, or whoever he is, from there. His original name was Herman Foley, but then he changed it to Kruger when he got out of prison the first time. I think that was a smart move. It had to be tough in prison with a name like Herman Foley. I bet they called him Herman the German."

"Well, okay." I wasn't sure how to respond to that piece of speculation.

Igor posed another question. "The woman... Jeanine Faraday. Do you think she knows rest of secret in message?"

I offered my thoughts. "She might. I wonder if Kruger took whoever Grande was in... or we are supposed to find Grande and take him or her in... and then who is Pas? The woman might know. From what I hear, she is very capable at pillow talk."

It certainly looked like Johnny turned a little red.

Tucker asked, "Do you think the tracker we had on her is still working?"

"Probably not. But why not check? I'm good with tech. I'm not a Luddite like you guys."

I flipped on the finder app on my phone. I had a solid hit on her house. I held it up for the others to see.

Tucker blurted out, "Holy crap, she's still at home."

I was shocked too. "I never would have guessed. I figured she blew town. Maybe she's still trying to find the cash."

Igor grunted, "We find woman, we find secret to money."

Johnny reluctantly agreed. "Igor's right. We need to go get her... but... I should probably work the outer perimeter. No sense blowing my cover."

I laughed. "I think all the blowing is over, pal. You can cover us."

"Kiss my ass, Becker. That's not funny."

Igor chortled, "Yes, funny. I don't speak good English and Igor think funny."

Dedd decided to shut up.

I gave orders. "You guys take the front. I'll come in from the alley. Johnny covers us. We need to talk to her. No rough stuff. I think we can cut a deal and get this message deciphered. She wants cash. She's not stupid and not violent."

"Define violent," Johnny grumbled.

Tucker knew I was right, and he understood Johnny's reluctance. "Well, everyone keep their pants on and we'll be fine."

"Okay, let's roll," I said, quoting one of America's greatest heroes.

Twenty minutes later, we were set up. Worm waited in the car. Igor, Dedd, and Tucker took the front. Dedd took a cover position while Tucker and Igor went to the door. I took the back, approaching from the alley.

I move quietly for an old man. I had my forty-five in my hand at the low-ready. My eyes were good enough for the light we had. Night vision equipment wasn't necessary if you were careful.

Kruger wasn't careful.

He accidentally bumped a trash can causing a stray black feline to caterwaul loudly as it sprinted away from the intruder to its lair.

He slung a round my way.

I dove into the dirt on my belly, landing hard with my gun out in front of me. "Drop it, asshole."

Here's the thing about an alley. It can be in an upscale neighborhood in a resort community, or it can be in the middle of a dirty inner-city downtown block. It doesn't matter. You can still get killed there. It was a lesson I almost forgot.

I saw the flame and heard the spit of a suppressed handgun as Kruger ripped off two more rounds in my direction. They were high and to the left.

I rolled to my right and found an old barbecue grill someone had abandoned. It was the old iron kind they used to make that weighed a ton. It was as good a cover as I was going to find.

I shouted, "Herman, you pussy! Drop your weapon or I'll kill your dumb ass right here and now."

I thought those words sounded particularly bad ass, but he still just kept shooting at me.

I heard him shout back after his volley, "I just want the woman... and don't call me Herman, you dick."

"Whatever you say, Herman." I popped off four rounds at him and did a tactical reload. I knew I missed, but they were just conversation shots, nothing serious. I was using subsonic rounds, so this was relatively quiet for a gunfight. It sounded more like a neighbor dispute. I didn't expect help from the cops. I was going to have to deal with this asshole myself.

I heard Kruger moving towards me, stumbling over shit, like big men will sometimes do in the dark. Goons often lumber during times when treading lightly is the key to survival. I used that information and fired two more rounds at the sound. The son of a bitch was so big, it would be hard to miss.

I heard a grunt and then a body hit the ground hard. I think the technical term is 'thud.'

"Becker, you asshole," he moaned in the dark.

I must have hit him pretty good.

A sound, similar to a deer crashing through the woods at a dead run, came from my left. I almost fired but realized was Johnny running hell bent for election with his gun in his hand.

"You okay, Becker?" he asked.

"I'm fine. I'm just having a chat with old Herman."

"You don't look fine."

"Shit."

I just realized I took one in the belly fat. I guess the adrenalin must have numbed it before. Now I felt it.

Johnny was anxious as a dog on a scent. "Do you mind if I kill him? I don't mind doing it. You know, if it's okay with you."

I thought that was a little weird. "Let me talk to him, Johnny, and we'll see."

We did a tactical approach and found Herman or Kruger or whatever he calls himself now, rolling on the ground with a big hole in his belly.

I pulled out the little flashlight I carry on my key ring and examined him. Damn. He was an enormous brute. Scary looking. Mean... but not too tough at the moment with that big patch of red staining his shirt.

"Kruger, I'll call an ambulance if you tell me where the money is," I offered.

He was still defiant. I don't think his brain registered the gravity of his current situation. "I don't know. All I know is there's supposed to be some message. The woman might know what it means. I just want the woman and I'll leave. I'll let you live."

Dedd grabbed him by the front of the shirt and pulled him in close to his face, which was quite a feat of strength, considering Kruger's size.

"Look asshole, you ripped off my client. You tried to blow up South Beach. You killed Schuster... admit it."

"I did... but I can split this money with you. It's forty million dollars. Do you know how much that is?"

Dedd did the calculations in his head. "It's forty million dollars?"

I noted a confused expression on Kruger's face. He's clearly not used to debating with Johnny Dedd. Specificity is the key.

Kruger responded. "Uh... yes... that's correct... but we can split it. We'll all be rich."

I'd heard enough to know that Herman-Kruger-scary-guy was of no further use to us. "Johnny, get him on his feet."

Dedd obediently helped Kruger up. He stood shakily.

"So Becker, we have a deal?" Kruger asked, misreading my intent.

My face grew taut with the inner rage that all cops keep

bottled up inside, rarely venting, bubbling just underneath the surface. Mine had been locked down for most of forty years. All the hatred and bitterness from everything I saw and did during my career seethed to the surface. Every act of senseless violence I cleaned up after evil people like Kruger destroyed lives was still fresh in my memory... every family member I consoled. Every death message I delivered. All of it. It is a never-ending battle to restrain this darkness that lives deep in the soul of every old cop who survived a career. But I had no intention of fighting it this time. He murdered Schuster. He shot me. That was enough.

I growled, "Here's the deal, maggot. You freely chose to take a walk down bullet alley tonight. You chose that all on your own. But you need to know...eventually that walk is a one-way trip. I don't give a black damn about how tough you think you are. Eventually they *will* get you. Tonight wasn't my night." I gestured with my shoulders to my associate. "Tonight wasn't Johnny's night." I gazed into Kruger's eyes with my own dead eyes, the thousand-yard stare, taking in a slow breath and releasing it before continuing. "It looks like tonight is *your* night, Kruger. It's your night to die." I paused and locked my gaze into Kruger's disbelieving face. "Cover your eyes, Johnny. I don't want any witnesses."

Kruger got the message. He started to scream something. I think it might have been '*Wait!*'

I lifted the Sig and popped him between the eyes. His head snapped back, and he fell flat on his back into the dirt with a dull thump. The case could be made that he was coming at me, presenting an immediate threat to my life. I could get people to believe that, considering the angles and all the other shit crime scene guys calculate on bullet trajectories, would back it up. Those who decide the fate of vigilantes would have no choice but to write the shooting off as justified, even if it was murder.

Johnny was grinning.

I was cooling down.

Then I slumped down.

"Becker!" Dedd shouted at me.

There was no need to shout. My hearing was fine, and the bullet wound to the gut didn't damage my ability to listen.

Johnny went all '*first aid dude*' on me. He pulled a flask out of his pocket. "It's vodka. Pour it on the wound."

I did as directed.

"Let me look."

I didn't argue with him.

"Becker, it's a deep graze."

"I think the bullet is still in there, Johnny. You have a pocket knife?"

"Yeah."

"Give it to me."

I used the borrowed knife to nudge the bullet out of the shallow wound cavity. The round was barely under the surface, was more like a zit under the skin than a bullet. God, I love middle age spread.

Johnny approved of my field surgery.

"We can super glue that mess together, Becker. Should be fine. It's just gonna hurt, so drink the rest of the vodka."

Again, I did as directed. But I doused the wound again first.

I felt a little better already.

"Help me to my feet, Johnny. Let's go in and talk to Faraday."

We walked around to the front of the house. The door was open and the rest of the guys were already in the living room, talking to Faraday. Johnny waited outside.

The conversation appeared to be an eternal game of cat and mouse. They were taking their time. It was taking too long. I'd been shot and I want to go home.

It was time to get to the point.

Faraday was on the couch, dressed in gorgeous black silk loungewear that completely revealed the secret of how she seduced and shook down all the old rich guys in town. She appeared relaxed, in charge, and smoking hot. I shouldn't have sent boys to do a man's job.

I took over.

"Tucker, find some super glue. I sprung a leak." I pulled my coat back so he could see the blood on my shirt.

Faraday was finally helpful. "There's some in the kitchen drawer by the stove, sweet cheeks."

Tucker disappeared into the kitchen. I sat down across from the woman of the hour.

"Jeanine, I'll agree to give you ten thousand dollars, and keep your name out of all of this shit, if you help me decipher a message. Otherwise, you go down for conspiracy and murder. I'll make it stick. I want a deal and no bullshit. You can go back to working geezers for gold after this and there are no hard feelings."

I knew that there was no sense in trying to scare her. A straight up deal might work though.

She considered my pitch, then spoke. "Becker, I wish you weren't a potential mark. We could own Florida if we worked together." Faraday casually shook a cigarette out of a pack and lit it. She took a long drag and blew smoke in my general direction.

Was her move seductive? Yeah, very seductive.

It didn't work.

Tucker returned. I grinned while he squeezed some glue into my wound. Tucker pressed the hide together over my fat and held it a few seconds until it sealed up well enough to get by.

I countered Jeanine's offer. "No thanks, baby. You're too much woman for just one man. I plan on soaking up some social security money before I check out. I might die with a smile on my face if I got in bed with you, figuratively speaking, of course."

"Of course," she said as she demurely crossed her legs in the other direction, ladylike, but sexy as hell.

I continued my point. "But I have a feeling you might kill me the first day. Kill me in a very nice way, but I'd still be dead." It was my turn to light up a smoke. "A man my age can only take so much."

She grinned. "You're right. And I have been working cons long enough to know when I played my last card. Let's see your message, Becker. For ten grand, I'll work for you."

I put the copy of the note down in front of her. I could see the wheels turning as the little asshole squirrels in her head spun the cage that makes her brain work.

Who am I kidding? She's probably smarter than all of the rest of us put together.

If I am found dead by suspicious circumstances, call Becker and tell him it was those guys from California. He will find them. Take in Grande, get to Pas.'

A few seconds passed, then a smile etched the corner of her mouth.

"Becker, did you ever get sick of his stupid Airplane movie quotes?"

"Yeah, it got annoying at the first one."

"Did you know he had a boat?"

"No... it doesn't surprise me, but I didn't know it."

"It's docked in that little marina by your house. He just used it to hide stuff on. Sometimes he'd take a woman there."

"Wait... you know where I live?"

'If Boris knew, I knew, honey... so, yeah. I know where you live."

"So, what about the boat?"

"It has a name... Macho Grande. The note doesn't want you to take anything... the *take*, or the score from California, is in the Macho Grande. And it's probably twenty-five yards from your back deck."

"Holy shit!" I was surprised. Not a lot surprises me anymore. I had difficulty processing the feeling.

"And Pas?" She asked, knowing she had the answer.

"Yeah."

"Pas is for Pasadena. He has a kid there. He wanted someone to take the score to his kid in Pasadena. The message is simple if you have some context. Have Becker take out the guy who killed me, who in this case is Mr. Kruger from California. The take is in the Macho Grande, find it and get it to my kid in Pasadena. It's as simple as that.

"No shit?"

"Yes, shit, handsome… all you have to do is walk out your back door and pick up forty-million dollars."

I grinned back at her. "If that's legitimate, I'll be bringing you your ten thousand tomorrow. We good?"

"We're good, sugar…" She eyeballed Igor. "Hey big stuff, how about going on a date to celebrate getting your money back."

Igor might not be a master of the English language, but evidently, he knows bullshit when he hears it. He replied, "I just get money back. I no want to lose again, or give to you. Nice try, woman. I prefer babushka… Can be trusted. You… not so much."

I saw Tucker and Dedd look at each other and mouth the word *babushka*. Obviously, they didn't know what it meant.

I snorted at Igor's response. Faraday winked at me. She's growing on me. I had to admit the old broad was charming as hell for a felonious con artist.

I wrapped up our little meeting of the minds. "I don't blame you for trying, Jeanine. We'll be in touch. Let's go, gentleman…. Worm, you too."

With that, my team of international immortals slowly walked to our cars, doing everything we could possibly do to create an image of calm and collected professionals, at least until we were out of Faraday's sight. Then we drove like maniacs to my place, whooping and cheering all the way.

CHAPTER 13

I might be old, but I can still cover thirty yards as fast as anybody before I drop dead of heart failure, whether I'm shot in the fat or not. I sprinted through the house and out to the extended dock at the edge of my place the led to the marina. I pretty much forgot about the bullet wound. A deep graze hurts, but it doesn't really incapacitate you unless you die.

I crossed over and turned a corner.

There it was.

The Macho Grande, named after some bullshit catch phrase from a stupid movie.

It was an older pocket cruiser, maybe twenty-four feet in length, with an eight-foot beam, but in excellent shape. I had the cabin door unlocked with my picks in record time and stepped down into the interior of the vessel.

Where would Schuster hide forty-million? Boats have a million nooks and crannies for hiding stuff. There was a berth under the ladder leading down into the cabin. I crawled back in it and saw three very large foam coolers. Could it be?

The coolers were the old style, maybe from the fifties or sixties, made of steel and thick foam material. They were secure as stagecoach strong boxes.

I picked those locks, too.

I opened the lid.

It was there. Stacked and packed. It had to be the whole forty-million in cash.

"Got it," I yelled back at my associates.

Dedd, Tucker, Worm, and Igor barely fit on the small craft, but they were all hopping around cheering. I was concerned we might sink the stupid thing. To be clear, the boat wasn't stupid. The name on the boat was stupid.

Someone would probably be calling the cops because of all the noise and flashlights in a marina that was supposed to be closed. After all, technically, this was a burglary.

I assigned the big boys to money transport duties. "Igor, Dedd… grab these coolers and hump them up to the house."

The guys obeyed for a change without pointless chatter and arguments. It was nice.

Ten minutes later, we were at my place on the speakerphone with the Tucker Investigations team in Los Angeles. Joe got them all on zoom calls from wherever they were at the late hour in California.

Tucker spoke for our group. "I'm happy to report that we have a full recovery of lost funds. Igor has agreed to stop killing people for the time being if we give him his share now. The case is a wrap, thanks to Becker."

I heard Mister Stump's voice come on the line. He was all business. "Photograph it, count it, and write it up. The client will charter a private jet for you out of Fort Lauderdale. We need you both back here with the money in eight hours. The banks will be open and we will wrap this up. Oh, and let Igor take his share, just make him sign for it."

"Done."

Vance spoke next. "Becker, I'm thinking about moving to Florida. Think you could use an associate? I'm tired of L.A. It's turning into a shit hole."

I saw Tucker's joy immediately turn to dismay.

Vance continued, "Joe, keep in mind you can come out anytime to see me. I'd like that."

"Really? I'd like that too."

I wish they'd just get together and stay together… but I had a feeling that wasn't happening.

Stump came back on the line delivering an ass chewing and some orders. "Hey! This is work, not the dating game. Tucker, get the money packed up and get your sorry ass back here. Becker, we will wire transfer you your cut and commission within forty-eight hours. Sound fair?"

"Fair enough. This turned out better than I thought it would. Thanks for dealing me in."

Joan came back on, "Maybe we'll make that memorandum of understanding we had for working this case a more permanent deal."

I liked the sound of that. "I'd be open to it. We can discuss it next week."

We said the usual string of meaningless but mandatory goodbye words and disconnected.

I thought about what was happening now. I took in a long, deep breath and let it go. A rude bastard might call a sigh. I call it breathing.

I guess I could finally get back to being lonely again.

Worm broke my pending state of depression. He spoke up with more than a little concern in his voice regarding a very legitimate question. "What about me?"

I thought about it for a second before I made an offer. I could just tell him *good luck*, but the guy took a bullet for some stranger in Miami just because. The world needs more guys like that. I could use a guy like that. People change. I sensed that Worm was due for a break.

"Can you clean?" I asked.

"Yeah, I was a janitor for a while in a hotel. I was good at it."

"Can you cook?"

"I was a grill cook for three years. I can cook anything."

I laid out an idea that I might regret later, but risk is life, and I could use a life right now. "Here's the deal. I could use a butler, but my butler needs to be a guy who can handle himself and watch my back. I also got a pal who has a diner down at the pier. If you want, you can work for me during the day and him on the night shift. I'll let you stay in the guest quarters here. It's got its own entrance. It's small, but you'll be fine."

"Hell yeah, Becker. I'd take that job. Can I do some private eye stuff, too?"

"Sure. Eventually. Just get healed up first, then you can go to work." I turned my attention to Dedd, "Johnny, you know where I keep the good stuff?"

"Yeah."

"Time to break it out. We have some celebrating to do."

Eight Hundred Dollars' Worth Of Booze Later

There are tearful goodbyes and hung-over goodbyes. We had the latter. Here's a pro-tip, never drink with a fucking Russian.

I gave the boys a ride to the airport. Igor went with them. Worm and I went back to the house, and I got him settled into his new quarters.

It was time for a forty-eight-hour nap.

EPILOGUE

Three days later I was fully recovered from my bullet wound, the hangover, and the physical beating my sixty-some year old body took during the Schuster case. My dead client had all his wishes granted except giving the money to his kid part. It wasn't his money and she wouldn't take it anyway. Who'd a thought Schuster would have a kid who was honest?

Case closed.

Farley and Spade were sent home to Los Angeles.

Nobody was trying to kill me.

Cops weren't interested in me as a suspect for anything. Dedd cleaned up the Kruger shooting. It took him about thirty minutes to toss the big bastard in a dumpster and close that part of the case. There wasn't even a police report taken.

I felt good, maybe even looking forward to the day.

I showered, steam then cold, put on my favorite black suit, popped my favorite hat on my head, and walked downstairs like I owned the joint, which I did.

I never had a butler before. Now I had a feeling it would work out fine. I should have done this years ago.

"Mr. Becker, coffee is ready. Your paper is out on the deck."

Worm stood at attention in the kitchen, sharply dressed in his new uniform, a short-sleeved silk Brooks Brothers casual sport shirt and some nicely pressed matching cotton shorts. Except for a tuft of red hair sticking out from under his new yachting cap, he looked pretty sophisticated. Full disclosure, I don't know what butlers are supposed to wear. My butler wears this.

"Take the paper up to my office, Mr. Worm." I took a sip of coffee. "I'll read it later. I'm going out for breakfast this morning.

"Yes, sir."

"Do you have a shift at the restaurant tonight?" I asked.

"Yes sir... Thom needs all hands this evening. Spring break crowd is coming to town."

I rolled my eyes at the thought of a hundred thousand drunk, horny teenagers destroying Fort Lauderdale. But in a few weeks, it will be a memory and our local businesses will make their yearly budget. It all works out.

"Permission to speak, sir?" Worm asked.

"Of course, Mr. Worm. What's on your mind?"

"I've been working a lot of hours. I've been staying busier than I've ever been."

"You want a day off?"

"No sir. I want to say thanks. Work has been good. I never had so much money in my pocket that was really mine. I didn't know what life without crime or drugs was. Everyone I knew my whole life was either an asshole or a mark." He paused and looked around my place, not like he was thinking of it as a target for a burglary, but with gratitude. "I like this life. I just wanted to thank you for not killing me or leaving me dead in the ditch someplace. Even if I deserved it. It means a lot."

He put his hand out. If I didn't know better, I would suspect he was suffering from some seasonal allergies. And they were contagious.

"My pleasure Mister Worm. My pleasure."

I shook his hand

I hopped in the Jag and put the top down. My next stop was the diner. Maybe I'd order something different today... nah, that's crazy talk... I decided to take a quick spin up ocean drive first. I lit a cigarette.

For the first time in a long time, I was in a good mood for no reason. I was just happy.

Maybe I'd call my old pal Maggie.

A cold beer might be just what the doctor ordered. And since Mr. Worm was working late, maybe we'd have a nightcap on the dock afterwards… and see where that goes.

The end

RECURRING CHARACTERS

Johnny Dedd appears in Dead Guy in the Alley, I Stomp on your Throat, and Murder Every Maggot.

Joe Tucker appears in Dead Guy in the Alley, I Stomp on your Throat, and Murder Every Maggot.

Mister Stump appears in Dead Guy in the Alley, I Stomp on your Throat, and Murder Every Maggot.

Joan Vance appears in Dead Guy in the Alley and Murder Every Maggot.

Deb Deluca appears in Murder Every Maggot.

ABOUT THE AUTHOR

Bronco Hammer

Bronco Hammer is the author of  over seventeen hard-boiled, extreme-action, mystery and thriller books. He is a retired law-enforcement officer and has been a rancher, treasure hunter, tech-entrepreneur, wild-fire hot-shot crew member, and a bartender. His wide range of interests including trucks, boats, motorcycles, wristwatches, cigars, whiskey, beer, cars, horses, guns, sandwiches, and science. He can often be found attending happy hour someplace near his home at Coronado Island, California.

WHAT READERS
ARE SAYING

"Why do I read Bronco Hammer? Since I began devouring his tomes, my IQ now hovers around 200. I have grown to 6'5". Women flock to me naturally. Bourbon has become my adult beverage of choice and fedoras my hat of choice. I drive a truck that shouts testosterone, yet I stop to help little old ladies and any folks who are in need. And I do not have a cat." - Freeman Rockdale

"For high-end braining and quality used tires, you can't go wrong with Bronco!" - Jim Collins

"A scorching, gut-wrenching tale of murder, revenge and bad hairstyles. So good I bought a second copy for my grandmother - actually, I bought the second copy for myself because Gran borrowed the first and never returned it. It's that kind of a book!" - Greg Atkins

"Raw, gritty...just a good read. Bronco Hammer books are training manuals for real men and women. You can't read one and not be changed for the better. 'Murica!" - Rick Fowler

"In the darkened halls of Noir shines the faint light of desperate measures of desperate men, this is the Author Bronco Hammer back alleys." - Kenny Wilson

"Pure unadulterated action with a certain unfiltered style that keeps you guessing throughout the twists and turns of the plot.

An E- ticket ride from start to finish!" - Chris Wells

"Good book. Me like read. Better when wife read it to me. She read good." - Jeff Trapp

ACKNOWLEDGEMENT

Thank you to the amazing artist and brother in blue, Bunny Warren for deciphering the Australian language for me. You are the best, my friend. The errors you might find are mine alone. *(Full disclosure, I couldn't understand a lot of what he was telling me.)*

Thank you to those who contribute weapons information and knowledge to this story. Any errors or omissions regarding firearms or other topics in the final version is totally on me, not them. I now, in no particular order, formally induct you into the Bronco Hammer *League of Weaponeers*® and Dodgers of Gunfire (Also known as the L.o.w. D.o.g.s)… I salute you!

League of Weaponeers - Dodgers of Gunfire

Ronald Swart

Skip Redpath

Jeff Gordinier

Earby Markham

Roger Fenton

Kenny Wilson

Jeff Trapp

Steve Dayton

Aahdree Gee

John Rolfe

Durwood Kirby

Rick Ormandy

Scott Joseph

Durwood Kirby

Brian Pemberton

Tim Fife

Steve Bergh
Tony Holmes
Scott Long
Bill Richardson
Randy Lewis
Robert Loban
William Tullock
Tony Chamberlain
Mike Ratke
Randy Willard
Jeremy Young
John Laird
John Sheffield

Additional inductees will be added in future books in the event that I missed any of you this time. I've been day drinking, so in all fairness, I don't see how any oversight can really be my fault. Let me know and you will be recognized in the next one.

Also a special thank you Paul Kennedy, Ryan Van Dyke, and Sami Jo Fife for providing very much appreciated marketing support and advice.

A WALK DOWN
BULLET ALLEY

Becker will return... after breakfast